Olivia Brophie

and the

Pearl of Tagelus

Olivia Brophie

and the

Pearl of Tagelus

Christopher Tozier

Pineapple Press, Inc.
Sarasota, Florida

Inquiries should be addressed to:
Pineapple Press, Inc.
P.O. Box 3889
Sarasota, Florida 34230

www.pineapplepress.com

Library of Congress Cataloging in Publication Data
Tozier, Christopher.
Olivia Brophie and the Pearl of Tagelus / Christopher Tozier. -- 1st ed.
   p. cm.
Summary: "Young Olivia moves to the Florida scrub and finds much more than sand and scrawny oak trees. Caught in a battle for the fate of the universe, she slips down a tortoise burrow into the vast Floridan Aquifer where ancient animals thrive in a mysterious world. She learns the secret of a brilliant pearl and must use its power to discover her life's ultimate destiny. First in the Olivia Brophie series. "-- Provided by publisher.
ISBN 978-1-56164-519-0
[1. Adventure and adventurers--Fiction. 2. Animals--Fiction. 3. Magic--Fiction. 4. Witches--Fiction. 5. Pearls--Fiction. 6. Florida--Fiction.] I. Title.
PZ7.T673Oli 2012
[Fic]--dc23
                        2011036783

First Edition
10 9 8 7 6 5 4 3 2 1

Design by Shé Hicks
Printed in the U.S.A.

Contents

To Melissa for setting love aloft.
To Cheeto for fierce loyalty.
To my father for quiet fire.
To the bears in the woods
just beyond the highway lights.

1

Pancakes to Waffles

There aren't many ways of saying it and the whole thing seems overly complicated, but put as simply as possible, Olivia Brophie's father did not want her around anymore.

This really should not have been a big surprise under the circumstances. In fact, her whole life started spinning out of control three weeks ago on her tenth birthday. A plain brown package arrived with no card, no return address, and strangely enough, no stamps. It was addressed simply to "Miss Olivia Brofee." No one *ever* called her "Miss" and clearly the sender didn't know her well enough to spell her name correctly.

"A secret admirer," Dad quipped, his eyes sparkling.

"No way," Olivia shot back. But the thought of it fired her cheeks so hotly she considered not even opening the box. Perhaps she should have just tossed it with the junk mail into the garbage. It was probably another dish detergent sample anyway. Even as she decided that was exactly what she should do, her thin fingernail worked its way inside the brown paper seam and ran along its edges to the corners.

As she opened the meticulously taped box, the smell of bananas and smoke exploded through her nose like a swarm of yellowjackets. Olivia stumbled backwards for a second before looking into the box. Inside sat a single red barrette. It looked old. Very old. Tiny gems encrusted its delicate surface in the pattern of miniature flowers and a single bumble-bee. As soon as her fingers picked it up, Olivia swore she saw a pink spark zip above her head and out the screen door. Her little brother Gnat was standing next to her — his own hands twitching as she opened the present — and he didn't say a single peep so, at the time, she figured the banana smoke made her see stars.

"Who sent me this?" Olivia wondered aloud. "It's . . . it's beautiful." As she turned the barrette in her hand, the sparkling bumblebee flew from one flower to another.

"My little one . . . all grown up . . . soon to be married," Dad wailed, rubbing pretend tears from his cheeks.

Gnat chuckled and wiped his nose with the back of his hand.

Olivia slipped the barrette into her brown hair and turned sideways in the mirror to see it glowing up there like a hazel berry. That should have been the end of it. Life should have returned to normal.

But disturbing things started happening. For one, deer started sleep-ing in the yard. When Olivia walked outside, the deer nervously pawed the ground, but they didn't run away. One even followed her from the front yard to the back. When Dad or Gnat went outside, they all leapt over the fence and clattered down the neighborhood streets.

Because the deer ate all of their hedges, Dad became very interested in making aluminum pie pan scarecrows. He even bought all of the wind chimes from the hardware store and hung them from the trees, hoping the wind would blow.

Someone also started leaving corn muffins in their mailbox.

"Don't you dare touch or bite into any of those muffins," Dad ordered Gnat, who already had a muffin halfway to his mouth. He called the

police, but they said "no crime had transpired."

Olivia started dreaming horrible dreams: dead frogs dropping from the trees, little eyeless dolls made of cactus spines, faces in her window, long fingers scratching words into the glass like "acu pira," "hurry up," and "I await you." That sort of thing. She soon learned that keeping the barrette in her hair while she slept would keep the nightmares away.

When she woke up the first morning of summer break three weeks later and shuffled downstairs for breakfast, she knew right away that something else was wrong. Something changed. Something worse than nervous deer and nightmares. Dad didn't pour himself a cup of coffee. He didn't pop his head through her door to wake her by saying "Time to get up, Butterfly." He didn't even walk out to the end of the driveway for the morning paper. He just stood in front of the kitchen window, looking out at the enormous cottonwood tree in the backyard. The leaves twitched with every slight breeze. Fawns stretched in the dappled light. It would have been a perfect morning if her life wasn't about to be ruined.

He tried to make it sound like a summer vacation, but no one packs *all* of their clothes and toys for a vacation, do they? Besides, he wouldn't look her in the eyes when he told her, "I did my best. I just need this." He didn't look like her father at all when he said it. His eyes were blanks, his mouth, even his skin looked different. He looked like a stranger.

"But why? I don't want to go. I can stay at Katie's," Olivia begged, giving her best gimmie-face that always worked on Dad. Only this time she wasn't faking it.

"I'm sorry, but you have to understand. I will come get you as soon as I can," he said.

"Can't we call Mom? In an emergency?"

"You know we can't do that," Dad snapped.

Mom was overseas in Iraq fighting in the war. The 147th Aviation Battalion. Mom had served in Iraq almost half of Olivia's life, most of what she could remember. Olivia had a cloth patch stitched with a red and tan hawk holding an arrow. The patch meant she was an honorary member of The 147th.

They were only allowed to talk on the phone the first of each month. Today was May 5th. They talked just a few short days ago and Mom had said nothing about anyone getting kicked out of the house. Olivia wished hard that it was the first of June so she could put an end to this craziness, but that seemed like years away now.

She listened to her father calling Aunt and Uncle Milligan from around the hallway corner. He covered his voice as he talked into the phone.

"Please come as soon as you can. The kids are excited. No . . . they don't know . . . Yes. We are still in the same place."

"Who said you get to decide?" Olivia screamed before Dad hung up the phone. "We've never even met them. They are probably freaks."

"That's enough," Dad sighed.

She stormed upstairs.

Gnat sprawled upside down in bed wearing his headphones and playing a video game. He happily believed Dad about their "surprise" vacation. Olivia certainly wasn't going to tell him the truth. He was only six years old. He was short, annoying, and almost always had candy in his mouth. His brown hair sat loosely high above his huge forehead. Gnat played video games constantly. He rarely spoke, but when he did, it was something like "Level Three!" or "Mega-blaster!" causing the adults around him to simply shake their heads and stare dumbly at him. Occasionally, he stood up and screamed at the top of his lungs with the most incredibly loud, whining sound — and for no apparent reason.

A few days later, Olivia was peeling the crust off a bologna and ketchup sandwich when she heard a crash outside. She ran to the front door. A long, turquoise car pulled into the driveway. It looked forty years old. The tires smoked, and something definitely burned under the hood. Olivia read some faded lettering that had been removed from its side years ago. It said, "Milligan's Exotic Citrus." The back of the car was jammed to the roof with tools, pillows, and clothes. Deer scattered in all directions.

A tall man with a graying beard jumped out of the driver's seat and yelled like he was mad about something. Out of the passenger door emerged a bright red woman. Various cups, napkins, pens, coins, magazines, maps, sunglasses, and what looked to Olivia like a brass trumpet fell out onto the driveway. That old car was so stuffed with junk that it exploded out of every door and window. Olivia heard the red woman screaming, "I told you! I told you!" Olivia ran to her room and slammed the door.

When she saw them next, they had obviously resolved their fight. Aunt in particular had a very kind, round face. She had the same curly brown hair as Olivia. And the same brown eyes. But she had freckles. Lots of freckles. She leaned over Olivia. "Are you ready to move . . . I mean visit Florida, Olivia? I'm your aunt!" she said with a gravelly voice.

Olivia turned over in her bed. "I'm not going anywhere in that piece of junk."

"Come on. We'll have fun."

Olivia didn't respond.

"We can go to the beach whenever you want. And Disney World is just a short drive away. Don't you *looove* Florida?"

"Ugh," Olivia grunted.

Uncle came inside to get her bags. Olivia snuck a peek. He looked like a ferret on hind legs. The top of his ungroomed head almost scraped against the ceiling. His tiny eyes darted around the room. His gaunt cheeks were wrinkled by something other than time. Maybe too much sun. Or too much worrying. He picked up almost all of her bags in one armful.

"We'll give you a few minutes," he said, signaling Aunt with his head to leave.

"You can give me a few years for all I care."

Uncle frowned.

Olivia suddenly missed her house very badly. Her closet was empty. Her drawers were open. Everything seemed quiet and hollow. She had never even been over the border to Minnesota or Illinois, much less Florida. Someone tapped softly on her door.

"Hey, Butterfly. I just want to say goodbye."

"You never even told me why." Her voice was almost too weak to say anything.

"I can't explain it now. It's complicated. Adult stuff. Just go with your aunt and take care of Nathan. I'll call you in a few days."

"I don't even like them. They're weird. I think Aunt smokes," she said, knowing that Dad didn't want her anywhere near a smoker.

"She quit smoking years ago. They aren't so bad. They're funny. You'll have a great time," he said, leaning over to hug Olivia. He said it in a way that really meant "No argument." She buried her nose into his shirt.

She never liked the sour smell of the pine sawdust he always had in his clothes from working the pulping yards, but she didn't mind it so much this time. He didn't hug her as hard as he usually did. His hands dropped faster than normal.

"Dad. Dad, don't make us go. Please," she said with tears running down her cheeks, "give Mom our phone number." But he was already walking out the door.

"I love you," she whispered.

Olivia couldn't figure out how, but Uncle crammed all of their stuff into the car and still had enough room for them to sit. Barely enough room. She squeezed herself into the back seat next to a finch cage filled with socks. On the floor, she shoved a miniature vacuum cleaner to the side with her feet. Olivia was convinced that the first time they turned left or hit the brakes, the entire wall of junk would bury her forever.

Dad didn't watch them leave. He didn't wave. He stood out back by the cottonwood tree.

And that was the last time Olivia saw Sun Prairie, Wisconsin.

Olivia stared out the window. Gnat sat next to her making faces at the other cars in between levels on his video game. Lips smacking on a caramel, his fingers jumped around methodically over the game's buttons for hours. She could hear the laser sounds blasting through his headphones. "He's going to be deaf before he turns six. And toothless," she thought.

Uncle tried to tell funny stories. He kept looking in the mirror to see if she was smiling. Aunt kept asking her if she was comfortable.

"Do you need anything? Can we get you something?" Over and over and over.

Olivia wanted to scream "NO already!" She wanted to scream loudly, like an adult, so they would take her seriously. But she didn't move a muscle. She simply stared out the window. She pressed her forehead into the glass. After one hour, her forehead hurt. After two hours, she couldn't feel a thing.

Olivia didn't want anyone to know she could hear them, or see what they see, or think any of this was acceptable. Once, she even held back a sneeze until she felt her head would explode. The thought of someone saying "Bless you!" or "Gesundheit!" if she actually *had* sneezed made her sick to her stomach. She watched the landscape pass by as they drove south, pressing her forehead harder and harder into the glass.

There were prisons in Illinois with names like "SuperMax" and "Ten Towers." They passed a dinosaur made from tractor parts, some mountains, and a waterfall. In Kentucky, she heard that there were a lot of horses; there were billboards that said so, but she didn't see a single one, not even a pony. One town in Georgia had a giant peach standing high on top of a pedestal. She thought there mustn't be a single place in that flat town that couldn't look up at any time of day and see that peach up in the sky.

At some point along the way, Olivia was not quite sure where, all of the pancakes turned to waffles. All of the apples turned to pecans. The Holsteins in the fields turned to Brahmans. The lilacs vanished. The birds grew larger than any bird she had ever seen and they stalked the roadside ditches for frogs.

They stopped at a gas station that looked like an old nineteenth-century plantation, at least on the outside. Behind the two-story columns was an enormous store containing every variety of jam known to mankind. Gnat ambled through the candy aisle filling a little paper bag with exotic sour balls and novelty chocolates. He beamed with excitement. They sold candy by the *pound!*

Olivia walked to the rear of the store, past the preserved alligator heads and rubber tomahawks. She was eating a fresh praline that she bought with her own money and it was pretty good. Suddenly, two men hustled her through a back door behind the plantation. One man covered her mouth so hard she thought she wouldn't be able to breathe. Olivia kicked and squirmed. She slipped out of their hands but before she could take a step, they grabbed her again. Their eyes darkened like pieces of coal. As hard as she struggled, they didn't even budge. The man behind her grabbed a fistful of her hair and pulled her head back. Tears streamed down her face. She was too scared to scream anymore. The second man leaned closer. He stunk of hair grease and old popcorn. He grabbed her by the chin and forced her head first to one side then the other.

"There must be some mistake," he scowled. "She doesn't have the mark."

"There is no mistake," the shorter man said. "Let me see." They traded places, only this time the greasy-haired man didn't grab her hair.

"Maybe you are right," the short man said perplexed, straightening up. "How can that be?"

Olivia saw her chance. With all of her strength, she stomped her heel on top of the greasy man's foot. With a yowl, he released her and she darted through the door back into the store. She heard the door click safely shut behind her as the men tried to force their way in.

"Oh! There you are, sugar," Aunt announced from halfway across the store. "Are you ready to get going again?"

Olivia wiped the tears from her cheeks. She had been crying for the last day and a half anyway, so no one really noticed these tears fell for a different reason. She knew she should have those men arrested, but she was so confused about *everything* right now.

She nodded her head and sped for the car. She saw the two men get into their white minivan and drive off. The short one stared at her with his black eyes.

"We are almost in Florida," Uncle announced, cramming Gnat into the back seat and quickly shutting the door to keep him from falling out. "It will be nice to be home again."

Back on the interstate, Olivia watched the wind pulling last year's cotton up from the fields. It floated like snow against the windshield. Uncle called it "orphan's cotton." Aunt punched him when he said it.

And then, finally, she saw the great and glassy sea. Olivia had never seen the sea before. Or palm trees. The closest she had come was on Palm Sunday when stern Pastor Kwashanski handed everyone a piece of palm frond to wave in the air when he gave the command after the Invocation. Although it seemed an odd thing to do in church, Olivia thought she would like a place like Florida where the palms waved in the air all year long.

Olivia's eyes grew big. She saw something silver jump just beyond where the waves were turning white.

"It's beautiful isn't it?" Aunt whispered over the seat. Olivia turned away so she couldn't even see Aunt out of the corners of her eyes.

Uncle pulled the old blue car over and yelled, "Everyone take off your shoes!" and the next thing Olivia knew he was running down the dunes toward the water. A trail of junk followed him. He left the keys in the car and the door open. There was a great commotion as Aunt pulled off her sandals and ran after him squealing. Gnat waddled along behind with his headphones still on and the cord dragging on the sand.

"This is stupid," Olivia said loudly in the empty car. She looked down the highway for the white minivan. Nothing. It felt good to be alone after being cooped up with these oddballs for so long. She took off her shoes and walked toward the beach. The sand burned her feet. Gnat was kneeling on the sand and sticking his fingers down a crab hole. Aunt and Uncle splashed each other in the waves. Olivia walked to a quieter spot down the beach and let the water wash over her burning heels. She watched each sparkling wave rise up clear as glass then foaming white as it crashed down.

A ship chugged away on the horizon getting smaller and smaller. Maybe it was sailing to Bombay or Jakarta or Timbuktu or Iraq. Olivia thought about what might be on the ship. Probably cabbages or blue jeans. Maybe the ship carried spies to the war. She thought something on the ship might find its way over the enormous ocean to her mom.

Olivia looked down at her feet and saw a pale, pink shell the size of her fingernail rising up out of the sand. Its fleshy arm stretched and flexed to hold itself upright. Then another shell rose up. And another! Shells were rising out of the sand everywhere. Thousands, each a different color. Striped and spotted. Tangerine, violet, and rose. Pink, indigo, and chocolate. Olivia smiled. There were so many shells she couldn't even see the sand beneath them. She could feel them tickling up under her feet. Funny-looking shrimp washed up in the waves and sat down in the sand around her. They were all staring up at her as if *she,* Olivia Brophie, were something inexplicably wonderful that they had never seen before. Their tiny black eyes never blinked.

"Oh my," Aunt exclaimed from up the beach. Olivia spun around. Hundreds of white crabs lined up on the sand. Even worse, birds of every shape and size stood on the beach, all staring at her silently. While she had watched the ship, the birds had quietly landed behind her back: pelicans, skimmers, oystercatchers, laughing gulls, turnstones, terns, ringbills, sandpipers, plovers, sanderlings, willets, gannets, grackles. But to her, they were all nameless birds. They all just stood there, staring with their yellow and black eyes. Their beaks snapped at the wind. Feathers ruffled. Olivia didn't move a muscle. She suddenly didn't like the beach very much. She couldn't breathe.

"AAaaaYiiiiiiiiiii!" Gnat screamed like a very loud fire alarm and stood up with a large crab hanging from one of his fingers. All of the birds took off with a great cackling and cawing. The white crabs scurried to their holes. The shrimp rode the next wave out to sea. The shells — all of those purple, pink, and blue shells — disappeared beneath the brown sand.

Olivia ran to Aunt, "What is going on?"

"I don't know. I've never . . ." She frowned at the birds circling overhead. "Come on. Let's go home." Aunt put her arm around Olivia as they walked back up the hot sand.

"Florida is very strange," Olivia thought. She didn't realize that this was going to be the *least* strange day she would have for a long, long time.

2

Opals

The sun was going down as their rusty turquoise car bumped along a quiet highway. A dark swamp pressed in on both sides of the road. Cypress trees loomed over them. Palms swayed their enormous green fans. Everything was draped with thick curtains of gray hanging moss. Olivia watched for eyes in the dark water. She had heard somewhere that alligator eyes glowed blood-red at night. Gnat was sleeping next to her with his video game still on. They had turned west from the beach and now it seemed like they were light-years away from those shells and rude birds.

Lyonia, Florida, lies lost somewhere at the center of the state between the swamps and miles of orange groves. The small town looked exactly like Uncle's car, old and junky. Olivia saw an antique store, a post office, a hardware store, El Taco Loco, and a brand-new gas station. She also counted two ragged old dogs and six chickens. The post office had a banner hanging in the window that said "Black Bear Carnival—Aug 13." Cars and trucks packed into a place called Croakers on the edge of town. Olivia was so tired of riding in the car that she didn't even care how stupid the town looked.

Ten miles later, they turned down a sandy road that was so overgrown she could hardly see it from the highway. It looked to Olivia like they were being swallowed by the trees.

"Are we here?" Gnat asked.

"This is our driveway," Aunt smiled.

"Finally," Olivia mumbled under her breath.

The surrounding forest was weird. The trees grew short and twisted. Most of them weren't much taller than Uncle. There was white sand everywhere, so much that it almost looked like they were back at the beach. Olivia saw cactus growing in the sand, and the tree bark was covered with red splotches.

But she was too tired to pay much attention. Finally, two days after it started, the horrible trip was over.

Then she saw the house. Old and broken, it squatted in the woods like a hobo. Some of it was brick, some stone. The wooden roof was patched with several old sheets of tin. There was no lawn, just lots and lots of white sand.

"You've got to be kidding."

"I know it isn't much," Aunt apologized. "It isn't what you are used to, but there is room for all of us."

A little fence made of crooked branches circled the house. Colorful bottles and glass ornaments hung all over the fence. Olivia heard them clinking in the breeze. A tiny old air-conditioner rattled and coughed on the side of the house. It could fall apart at any minute. It may have been evening, but the air felt like a summer greenhouse. The short trees screamed with insects who sounded very large and bloodthirsty. She could barely hear anything over their noise.

"Come on. Let's go inside and get ready for bed," Uncle said as he lifted Gnat from the back of the car.

The front door of the house opened and an angry dachshund tumbled outside barking at the top of his lungs.

"Baybeeeeee!" Aunt squealed. "We missed you widdle *widdle* bay-beee! Kids, I want you to meet Cheeto."

Gnat, safely cradled in Uncle's arms, shouted, "Incoming! Defensive shields up!"

Uncle joined in laughing, "Take that alien dog!"

Cheeto was long, red, and lean. He took things very seriously and he did not seem happy to see them. He ran around Olivia's feet sniffing and growling.

Olivia rolled her eyes. Suddenly bored with the newcomers, Cheeto ran off into the forest.

"Come back!" Gnat yelled.

"Cheeto doesn't trust anybody, not even Uncle. He will be fine," reassured Aunt.

If the car was full of junk, then their house was completely conquered by it. Bookshelves lined every wall. Piles of old magazines sat on the floor. There were countless artifacts, oddities, specimens, curios, totems, and geegaws sitting or hanging on every possible space.

"It sure is bigger on the inside than it looked outside," Olivia thought. There was a giant boulder taking up entirely too much room in the corner of the living room. The rock was taller than Olivia and four times wider. It must have weighed a ton.

"Your Uncle found that in the middle of the Orinoco River in Venezuela. He carried that darn thing out of the jungle fifty years ago," Aunt explained when she saw Olivia touching it. "He won't put it outside. I'll probably have to bury him with it."

Olivia couldn't imagine how one man could carry such an enormous rock through the jungle. She looked closer. It was filled with smooth chunks of shining multicolored nuggets embedded into the rock.

"Opals," Aunt whispered, smiling.

"Wait. Fifty years ago? How old is Uncle anyway?" But Aunt had already disappeared into the kitchen.

Olivia looked at the pictures on the wall: jungle waterfalls, a young woman in a bi-plane, exotic cities, and precarious poses on mountain-tops. One photograph showed two girls in the foreground with a boy swinging on a rope and dropping into a swimming hole. The two girls looked like they just got out of the beautiful blue water. One looked very familiar to Olivia.

And then it struck her. She hadn't seen the TV yet.

"Ummmm . . . Ex*cuse* me. Where is the TV?" Olivia asked loudly and with enough attitude that there was no doubt about her irritation.

From somewhere several rooms away, Aunt responded, "I'm sorry, dear. We don't have one. Maybe we can fix one of the ones in the garage."

"What?? How do you know what is going on in the world? Who doesn't have a TV? What do you do for fun?"

"We fix TVs."

"Just great," Olivia thought, "not only is there no TV, no neighbors, and no lawn, but they have to be smart alecks about it."

"Well, where's the phone? You do have one of those, right? I want to call Dad."

"Why don't you wait until morning," Aunt said more as a command than a question. "It's getting late."

"Can you at least tell me where my room is?" she said, rolling her eyes. She never wanted to come in the first place and these people didn't even have a TV. How would she watch movies or find out what was going on in Iraq? She felt her skin turning hot. No TV!

"Haaaarooooooold!" Aunt called out in an uncomfortably loud voice. "Haaaaarooooold! Where are you?"

"I'm coming, just a second."

"Why don't you answer?"

"I said I'm *coming*. Now pipe down."

"Don't you tell me to pipe down." Aunt's face turned bright red. She slammed the cupboard door. It sounded like something porcelain broke inside. "The kids need their stuff! Don't *you* tell *me* to pipe down!"

Uncle was just walking through with some bags, winked at Olivia, and said, "Follow me, Butterfly."

"Don't call me Butterfly," Olivia ordered.

"Huh?"

"Butterfly. Don't call me that."

"Follow me, Kumquat," Uncle smirked

"And don't bother bringing them all inside. You can take me home tomorrow," she mumbled as they walked down a long hallway. "This house keeps getting bigger and bigger inside."

Down at the end of the hall was a bright blue door. Uncle turned the old glass knob and walked in.

"Here you go! Good as new."

To Olivia's surprise, the room was surprisingly clean and bare. "What? No shrunken heads or stacks of magazines or giant boulders?"

Uncle chuckled to himself and walked out.

The bed looked like something an emperor would sleep in, the emperor of mummies. It must be five hundred years old. The large dark bedposts rose all the way to the ceiling. When Olivia jumped onto the mattress she sunk down low. It was like lying in a big pile of fluffy snow. She fell asleep before she even got her shoes off.

Aunt came in later. "Goodnight Olivia. Just knock on the green door down the hall if you need anything. The bathroom is the next room down. The room with a yellow door." She yanked Olivia's shoes off and pulled the sheets over her.

"Is that Mom in that picture on the shelf by Uncle's rock?" Olivia asked, half asleep.

"She was just a little older than you when that was taken."

"I'm still going home in the morning, you know. I'm not even going to unpack."

"I know," Aunt said, kissing her on the forehead. She left the door cracked.

Olivia stared out the window from the bed. The moon was shining brightly on the white sand. The bedroom windows were covered with dripping water on the outside, distorting her view of the forest. The cold, air-conditioned air caused dew to form on the glass as it contacted the hot humid air of the outdoors.

Olivia whispered, "Condensation," proud of herself for remembering a vocabulary word from school. She reached up and felt the red birthday barrette in her hair and fell back onto the soft mattress.

As her eyelids grew heavy and blurry, she noticed several tree frogs clinging to the wet window. They were walking and hopping along the slick surface. Their circular suction toes spread wide as they stepped gently, leaving intricate tracks in the dew. She could hear them calling to each other in their language of peeps, gargles, and burps.

"There are no frogs like that in Sun Prairie," she thought. She could hear Aunt and Uncle arguing in the living room. And for reasons that Olivia could not explain, she began to cry.

3

Hunting the Bobwhite Witch

To Olivia's relief, the cupboard overflowed with boxes of cereal. She had figured that the Milligans were going to make her eat Cream of Wheat or bran muffins or grapefruits washed down with cranberry juice. These old anti-TV hippies certainly wouldn't have anything good to eat. On the contrary, there were so many boxes of cereal she couldn't think of a single kind that wasn't in there. From behind the Frosted Flakes and Cinnamon Life, she pulled out the Froot Loops and sat down at the kitchen table. Gnat was already shoveling an extraordinarily large bowl of Cocoa Puffs into his mouth with an extraordinarily large spoon.

"Uh, . . . Gnat. Who said you get to eat so much sugar?"

He pointed his spoon to the other room, "Mothership."

"*She* is not your mothership. She is your aunt. Did you sleep all right?"

"Affirmative."

"Well, I sure did. That weird bed was . . . What is that?" she said looking out the window. There, in the sand outside, a red-, yellow-, and black-banded snake slithered from the house toward the forest. It carved a curving trail in the sand. Precisely following the trail left by the first snake, another snake came out from under the house. And another. A long line of snakes, nose to tail, slithered their way to the trees. Because they all followed the same track, the sand looked like only a single snake had passed.

Aunt leaned over the table. "Those are the coral snakes. They live under the house. Don't go messin' with them, they are very poisonous."

"They *live* . . . under the *house?*" Olivia stammered.

"For almost as long as we've lived here," Aunt said.

"Then why don't you kill them?"

"They haven't hurt anyone."

"Yet," mumbled Olivia. Still, she couldn't resist watching the colorful snakes as they ribboned their way in the sunlight.

"They will come back home before the sun goes down."

"Why do you have so many cereal boxes?" Gnat interrupted.

"Because we knew you liked cereal," Aunt responded.

That answer made sense to Gnat and he nodded his head as he pushed another spoonful into his mouth.

Olivia watched the last tail of the last snake disappear behind a pine tree. "I wonder where they are going," she said to no one in particular. "Maybe they have a job. I wonder what kind of kingdom they have underneath the house."

"I don't know, but listen to me, don't you go looking," Aunt said sternly. "I mean it."

"I'll bet their kingdom is filled with jewels and pretty little birds that they have charmed. I'll bet they have beds of silk down there." Olivia paused for a second and then stood straight up. "All right. I want to call Dad and have him come get me . . . I mean us — unless Cereal Freak wants to stay here. I'm sure he will love having no TV. Where is the phone?"

Aunt studied Olivia for a long time and then pointed to the phone on the wall behind a big jar of artfully arranged noodles.

Gnat looked up from the table with a chunk of cereal stuck to his chin. "What? No TV?"

Olivia grabbed the phone and stormed to another room where she stayed for several minutes. Then she returned the phone to the wall. "I left a message. He will be here this weekend."

Olivia threw her cereal bowl on the counter and ran outside to find the coral snake trail. It was already hotter at nine in the morning than it ever got in Wisconsin. The small trees in the dwarf forest were all twisted and contorted. Their limbs draped with long, hanging Spanish moss. Some taller pine trees growing in the forest looked a little more normal. Except they weren't normal. Every single one of them tilted at an angle as if a giant hand had come down from the sky and knocked all of them over. The entire forest floor consisted of white sand. The pathways around the crooked trees were white. White sand rippled where the breeze had tossed it. Olivia saw tiny, perfectly round holes bored down into the sand that looked like crab holes at the beach. She wondered what might live down there.

Most of the backyard consisted of Aunt's flower garden. Some flowers only opened in the morning light. Some flowers wilted and died as soon as the sun rays touched them. There were big, plate-sized blooms and long, hanging clusters. Pink pom-poms covered the ground, each tiny pink petal tipped with a yellow glob of pollen. Butterflies fluttered everywhere. She sat on a bench and watched the goldfish darting back and forth underneath the lilies in their pond. Fierce dragonflies perched on the giant fern fronds overhanging the water. They each sat for a moment, polished their giant eyes with their front legs, and then zipped back to the sky. Smaller damselflies fluttered closer to the surface of the pond. Their colorful bodies and dainty wing beats reminded her of ballet dancers. Olivia had always wanted to take ballet lessons like some of the girls in her class. Even jazz dancing. The only dance she knew how to do was polka. Polka dancing was fun and she could polka all night long at weddings. But *everyone* can polka, even Dad. No one would *pay* to see you polka. No audience would jump to its feet with excitement. She wanted to dance up in the air, with nice slippers, and violins, and flying silks. Just once, she wanted everyone to think that she, Olivia Brophie, was the most fantastic dancer in the world.

She looked up and saw Uncle on the other side of the yard. He was wearing a huge straw hat. Olivia almost yelled to him, but he seemed so busy that she just watched him slowly cross the yard. He carried a hammer and a very large birdhouse back to the fence by the trees. The birdhouse was as tall as he was. He had built it out of a hollowed-out log. The roof was covered with thick bark and peaked up into fine gables. A cross perched at the top of an elegant steeple. Twelve tall windows circled around the structure and each was painted to mimic stained glass. Sparkling crystals hung from the corners. It reminded her of a rustic cathedral or a log cabin church. Olivia could see that it had an extra-large hole cut into an arch for the birds to enter. Uncle found a spot on the fence that could support the colossal church and hammered it securely with three thick, silver nails. She ducked behind a big red hibiscus bush to get a better view. Uncle stepped back and looked up into the tops of the trees. The yellow morning sunlight glowed on the leaves as the mist rose up and disappeared into the sky.

"That old fool," Olivia thought, "he thinks the birds are just going to fly inside with him standing there."

She was about to step out from behind the bush and tell Uncle to back up if he wants the birds to come, but then she noticed something up in the trees. Something big shifted and stretched its legs. Olivia waited for some strange, stupid Florida bird to flap its wings. The only things she could see were oak leaves, pine needles, and branches. She squinted and tried to focus on the movement. Slowly, on wire-thin legs, an enormous walkingstick insect turned its long, skinny body around and started walking down the tree. Its body was ebony-black and shiny with two bright white stripes running along the back. She didn't think an insect could be this large. It looked big enough to carry a small dog up into the oaks. Its face, like all insects, was expressionless. But there was an air of peace and contemplation about it. It didn't freak her out at all like the roach she saw last night or the wasps that used to prowl the screen porch back home. How had she not seen it there before?

Suddenly, all over the branches, the leaves came to life. Hundreds of walkingsticks marched silently down to the birdhouse. Slowly. Deliberately. They stepped carefully among the shifting leaves. An ancient arboreal tribe emerged. Olivia held her breath. One by one, they lowered their heads into the opening of the new church and slid their long bodies inside. She heard Uncle speaking gently to them. His voice was a faint comfort on the breeze. "Yes, I knew you would like it. There, there. Yes, there is plenty of room for everyone. You will be safe, safe in here." A warm breeze blew. The bits of colored glass on the fence clinked like bells. Olivia closed her eyes, listening, oh listening!

Moments later she opened her eyes. Uncle was gone. Olivia stood

up from behind the bush, walked over to the walkingstick church and peeked into the darkness. All she could see was a tangled mess of black legs and antennae. A strange spicy perfume wafted out of the opening. It made her sneeze.

Somewhere in the trees, a beautiful musical note whistled. It wasn't a loud note, but in the quiet air it rang clear and sweet. *What could it be?* It whistled again. *What a charming sound!* It slid up like a question. Olivia took a step into the woods. She peered through the dwarf trees and palmettos, trying to find who, or what, it was. She started walking. The white sand slid softly under her feet. Another whistle. *It was coming from beyond that pine.* She walked faster. The whistler seemed to be moving away just as fast as she walked. Olivia's feet moved faster and faster underneath her. She just *had* to find out what was making that beautiful noise. She ran faster and faster. A sudden wave of fear swept over her. She couldn't stop. Something inside pushed against her muscles. Her legs were a blur. She had never run this fast in her life. It felt like the air was carrying her. Sweat soaked her clothes. She plunged through palmettos and cactus, their spines searing her skin. The oak branches scratched across her face. And then . . .

She stopped.

Exhausted, Olivia collapsed onto the sand, staring up at the blue sky. The only thing she could hear was her own heavy breathing. The whistling stopped.

"What was that all about?" she said to no one in particular. She looked to her side. There, on the edge of the brush, stood a brown bird the size of a chicken. Olivia tried to sit up, but she was so exhausted she couldn't move. Her arms and legs felt heavy as concrete. She could see twenty more birds standing behind it. Maybe more. The bird looked right into her eyes and tilted its head. It was contemplating her. A cold chill poured through her skin. She struggled to her feet. Wobbling, she yelled, "Go! Go!" and swung her arms wildly. A strange humming noise grew in her ears. It sounded like chanting from far away. It sounded like a screeching train, louder, louder until she thought her eardrums would burst.

"Hello? Are you OK? Wake up! Hello? If you don't get up the ants are going to get ya."

Olivia felt dizzy. She had passed out. She tried to open her eyes but the sun came rushing in. Someone was poking her side with a stick.

"Sit up. There are ants all over."

She swatted at the stick with her arm and sat up. Sand shook out of her messed up hair. The rude person poked her with the stick again.

"Knock it off," she snipped.

"Are you OK?"

"I'm fine," she said reaching down to her ankles. "Ouch!" There were cactus spines and blood all over her shins.

"Here. Let me help you up."

Olivia squinted up to see a skinny boy holding his hand out to her. He had light blond hair, a buzz cut, and tiny ears. In fact, he had the tiniest ears she had ever seen.

"Come on. Get up before you get bit," he said, grinning.

"What's so funny?" she snapped. Olivia could see that he had a bundle of wire flags and a notebook with him.

He reached down and pulled her up.

"Thanks. Did you see any birds standing around out here?" Olivia asked.

"Huh?"

"Birds. Brown birds. Size of a chicken. Did you see any?"

"Not really. I saw a cardinal just over there. Listen, my name is Doug."

"Oh. I'm Olivia. Thanks."

"Are you sure you are OK?"

"Not really. The weirdest thing just happened. There was this whistle and I couldn't find it and I ran farther and farther. . . ." Olivia saw the worried look on Doug's face. "Uh, forget it."

"What are you doing out here anyway?" Doug asked. "Here, have some water. Nobody comes out here without water." He handed Olivia an old tin canteen. The water tasted so sweet on her dried lips.

"I'm visiting my aunt and uncle. The Milligans. What are you doing out here?"

"I'm marking tortoise burrows for a school project."

"It's summertime. Isn't school out?"

"Yeah, well, it's extra credit. I'm monitoring all of the burrows that I can find out here. Where are you from anyway? You have a funny accent."

"I have an accent? Ha!"

"And you are wearing flip-flops. That ain't too bright."

"Listen, I wasn't planning on coming out here. Just point me the way to get back."

"How 'bout I walk with you. I have to find more burrows."

"Fine. You know, *you* are the one with an accent. Ouch! Those cactus spines hurt!"

"Yeah. Well you aren't supposed to mess with them. Just pick off the ones you can see. You are gonna have to get the little ones when you get home. Don't touch your eyes whatever you do. They'll have to pluck out your eyes if you get the spines in there."

Olivia leaned over and started pulling out the spines from her shins. Blood dripped down her legs. "What kind of forest is this anyway? It sure is weird. OUCH!"

"It's called scrub, and there's no other place in the world like it. It's what I'm doing my project on."

"I thought you were doing it on turtles."

"First of all, they are tortoises, not turtles. And second of all, I'm trying to find as many endangered species as I can out here."

"Well, Nature Boy, you can have it. There aren't even any pretty trees. And, the birds . . ." she stopped herself. "Let's just go."

They started walking back to her house. Olivia felt safer with Doug there, even if he was a little scrawny.

"So tell me, what are we looking for? Burrows?" she asked.

"Yeah, tortoise burrows. I'm putting a flag on each one and marking it on my map so I can find it later. Look. Here's one." He pointed to a large hole slanting down into the sand. It looked like something had been digging at it just a few moments ago. Olivia knelt down and peered inside. She could see a gray, scaly foot just on the edge of the darkness. Then, as if it could feel her eyes looking, it disappeared altogether into the depths.

"I think I saw one!" she said.

"Probably." Doug said. "All sorts of things live down in those burrows. Rattlesnakes. Gopher frogs. Indigo snakes. Mice. Even owls."

"Hmm. Did I tell you that twenty-five coral snakes live under my house, I mean, my aunt's house?"

"Considering we just met a minute ago . . . no. And I doubt that. Coral snakes are solitary."

"Shows you what you know, Nature Boy. I've seen 'em."

"Are you sure they aren't king snakes?"

"My aunt said so. Corals. That's what she called them."

"Well, they must just be under there hunting mice. They are solitary."

"You don't know it all. Hey, there's another burrow."

"And there's the tortoise over there," Doug pointed across the clearing. "Looks like a really old one." The tortoise's shell was a glossy gray color and elegantly sculpted. His head reminded Olivia of an old man. The tortoise was slowly chomping on a cactus.

"They eat those things?" Olivia exclaimed.

The tortoise looked up. Its beak was covered with red berries of some kind.

"Get 'em!" Olivia shouted and took off running.

"No, wait!" Doug shouted back.

Olivia sprinted across the sand, convinced that she had the old tortoise cornered, but it turned and bolted into its burrow with amazing quickness.

"You are never going to catch one that way, dummy. Besides, why can't you just leave him alone?" Doug continued his lecture. "It's a little-known fact that no matter how fast you run or how quietly you sneak around, you will never catch a tortoise that way. They are significantly faster than most people believe."

"That thing is fast," Olivia was still shouting, ignoring Doug. "I thought they were supposed to be slow. Gimmee a stick!" She peered down into the burrow. The burrow was so big that Olivia figured she could probably squeeze down there herself.

"No way. Just let him be. Besides, I just told you tortoises are fast. Do you have hearing problems?"

As she kneeled there, she could see the tortoise facing her down in the darkness. Olivia looked into his wise eyes. She reached down trying to grab him.

"Eh. I wouldn't do that. There might be rattlesnakes down there," Doug warned.

"Get up here, Mr. Gruffle," Olivia ordered.

"Mr. Gruffle?" Doug asked. Olivia could name anything. She always thought of the perfect name for even the most mundane of things. She is the one, after all, who named Gnat "Gnat" even if their parents refused to spell it with a G.

"Yeah, Mr. Gruffle." She looked at Doug like she wanted to add, "and do you want to make something of it?"

"Oooookay . . . put a flag on Mr. Gruffle's house, please." He handed her a red flag.

"You know, the animals sure are brave in Florida," Olivia said as they started walking again.

"I dunno," said Doug. "There are plenty of bears and panthers and rattlers out here and I never see them."

"And corals. Lots of corals," she responded with a smile.

"Yeah, for a solitary snake, I guess they are plentiful. You know, you never told me where you were from."

"That is because you were rude. I'm from Wisconsin."

"Sorry, I just never heard that accent before."

"It's all right," she said, pulling some leaves off a small tree next to her. "You grow up around here?"

"Yup. Just down the road."

"How many endangered species do you think are out here?" she asked.

"Well, the books say there are a bunch that haven't been discovered yet. My plan is to discover a new animal. I have as good a chance out here as anyone. You get to name it yourself when you discover one, you know."

"What are you going to name it?" Olivia asked.

"I don't know yet. I suppose it depends on what I discover," Doug responded. "I have ideas."

"Well what are your ideas?" Olivia was getting irritated.

Doug turned red. "I dunno. . . ."

"You should have seen those chickens back there. They were *definitely* weird."

"Looks like Dougie here has a girlfriend. The new Milligan girl." Three large boys and a girl stepped out from behind some bushes. Two of the boys were carrying shotguns.

"Oh geez," Doug said. "Come on, Larry, we are just walking through."

"How many people are walking around out here in the middle of nowhere?" thought Olivia.

Olivia noticed that Larry was starting to grow facial hair and it was coming in patchy. He was clearly a few years older than anyone else. Later, Doug explained to Olivia that everyone in Lyonia called Larry Mutch and his brother Richard "the twins" even though Richard was born two years later. Their Dad had held Larry back a few years so he would be bigger than the other boys on the football team. He hadn't held Richard back in school because he showed no athletic talent. In fact, he was particularly slow and clumsy. So the twins were in the same grade at school despite two years of age difference. No one dared argue with them over the issue.

Olivia learned the skinny boy's name was Cucumber Nevels and that his buddies called him Cuke. He was as devious as Larry was dumb. Doug told her that Cuke must have decided years ago that he would be friends with the biggest, meanest boys who would then protect him. Doug was sure he was also trying to get into the *Guinness Book of World Records* by growing the world's longest mullet. Begonia Salt was the girl. She never said much, but she didn't have to because she was on the football team herself, and not as a kicker but a linebacker.

"I'm Olivia," she said, trying to be nice. She hadn't learned yet that trying to be nice to this gang wouldn't help matters.

"O . . . liv . . . ee . . . uh," Cuke stretched out her name because he couldn't think of anything else to make fun of. "How you like being a Milligan? You know, everyone around here thinks they are freaks. You better be careful."

Olivia blushed.

"What are you guys doing out here anywhere? There is no hunting allowed. This is protected," Doug asked.

"None of yer business," Larry snipped. "But if it matters so much, we are huntin' the Bobwhite Witch."

"Who is Bob White?" Olivia asked, suddenly interested. The boys started laughing and slapping each other with exaggerated glee. Begonia didn't crack a smile.

"Who is Bob White? Bobwhite is not a *person,* Einstein. Bobwhite is a bird-witch, a cannibal bird-witch and we aim to kill her. Who is Bob White! That's classic!" Cuke snickered with his unnaturally high voice.

"You sure are dumb. Yer gonna fit right in with those Milligans," Richard said, getting right in Olivia's face.

"You know, you are the ugliest and smelliest thing I've seen in a while," Olivia shot back.

"Nobody talks to my brother like that," Larry lunged for her.

Doug stepped between them. "Leave her alone, Mutch." He felt braver than ever before. It surged through him like a wave. "She didn't do anything to you."

"Whoa! Look at Corcoran getting tough now!" Cuke smirked. "You aren't gonna cry for us today, Dougie Baby? Dontcha have a math class to teach or sumthin'?"

"Leave . . . her . . . alone," Doug repeated. He started to regret jumping in. Richard slowly walked behind him.

Larry stared at Doug for a moment. Richard was getting on all fours behind Doug's legs. "All right, Dougie. I won't mess you up in front of your girlfriend. Summer is a long time. Try not to step on any more cactus, Milligan. Let's go guys." Larry shoved Doug as hard as he could. Just as Doug stumbled onto Richard's back, Richard stood straight up, sending Doug end over end into the bushes. Begonia sneered and looked Olivia up and down as she walked past. Olivia swore she heard Begonia growl.

"Jerks," Olivia said when she was sure they were out of earshot.

"Geez. You almost got us killed," Doug said brushing himself off.

"I've never stood up to a bully before," Olivia could barely breathe.

"Me neither."

"What kind of name is Cucumber anyway?" Olivia chuckled, helping him pick up the scattered papers and flags.

"I dunno. If the Nevels had more kids, they would probably name them all after vegetables," Doug said.

"Like lettuce."

"Or cabbage."

"His younger sister Tomato and older brother Artichoke," Olivia laughed.

"The whole family is a salad."

"You ever hear of the Bobwhite Witch?" Olivia asked.

"It's just an old kid's story. There are no such things as witches. Those guys are just too dumb to know any better," Doug said.

"Well, what is it?" she asked, getting irritated.

"What is what?"

"The *story.*"

"It says that she can turn into a bobwhite whenever she wants and she has a covey of other bobwhites that follows her around. She steals babies, kills people at midnight, sneaks around your house at night peeking in windows, that sort of stuff. Hmmmm . . . here are some blueberries that the bears haven't gotten yet." He started picking the little berries and eating them. Olivia joined him. She didn't realize how hungry she was until the first few berries squished between her teeth.

"These aren't that great."

"Better than nothing," he said.

"So you don't think the Witch is real? I mean, she *could* be real. You don't *really* know."

"My Mom says it's nonsense," he responded. "Chasing fairy tales doesn't help me find a new species."

"What time is it anyway?" she just realized how late it must be getting.

Doug looked at his watch. "Four o'clock."

"Oh, no. I better get home. Aunt must be worried by now."

They started walking at a faster pace. It really wasn't such an ugly forest as Olivia had thought at first. In some places, clouds of rainbow-colored scarabs whirred up toward the sun. In some places, large blue birds flew in close to watch them walk by. One even landed briefly on Doug's head. Doug showed her the Vomiting Holly, a tree whose leaves make even the most robust man vomit uncontrollably for hours and was once worshiped by the Indians. He showed her the poisonous coontie plant that those same Indians made their mealy bread out of.

"How do you know all this stuff?" she asked.

"You do realize that I'm a nerd, right?" Doug said, more of a statement than a question.

"I . . . I guess so," Olivia felt guilty for saying it. Doug smiled a little.

They walked quietly for the next fifteen minutes until reaching the Milligans' fence.

"Thanks for helping me, Nature Boy. You know, my Dad won't be here to pick me up for a few days. I wouldn't mind helping you find more tortoise burrows tomorrow. I mean, if you want."

"Yeah. That would be cool. Meet me at Mr. Gruffle's tomorrow at ten," he said with a wink.

"OK. Deal."

Olivia snuck through the fence and ran to the side of the house. She found the curving trail of the coral snakes in the sand. From out of her pocket, she pulled a handful of blueberries and left them right in the middle of their path. She heard thunder and it started to rain even though the sun was still shining. As she ran inside, she looked back to the place in the forest where Doug left her. The raindrops were shining in the sun, igniting the trees with a billion sparkling lights.

"Excuse me young lady," Aunt started scolding her as soon as she walked in the door. "Where have you been?" Cheeto bolted out of the next room, yelping uncontrollably. He crowded around her, sniffing.

"I was just walking around," Olivia lied. "Hi, Cheeto! You remember me!"

"You were just walking around for six hours? Listen, don't go running off like that without telling us. I was worried sick. Oh my! And look at your legs!" she noticed the dried blood. "Come into the bathroom. We can fix that."

In the bathroom, Olivia jumped up on the countertop. Aunt grabbed a tweezers and started pulling the little cactus hairs from her skin. Her legs were itching like crazy.

"You didn't touch your eyes did you?" Aunt asked.

"No. Doug told me . . ." she paused, knowing her secret was out. "Doug told me not to."

"Doug, huh?" Aunt asked, smiling. "Doug Corcoran?"

Olivia nodded.

"Well, he's a nice boy. I know his mom from the library. Just be careful if you are going to be running around out there. And don't go without telling me or your uncle again."

"All right," she said rolling her eyes. "Ow! Hey. Did Dad call?"

"I'm sorry, hon. Not yet."

"Well, he will tonight when he gets home from work. Ow! Where's Gnat?"

"*Nathan* hasn't left the couch or his video game all day."

"Figures. Right now, I wish you had a TV."

"There, I think I got all of them," Aunt said as Olivia jumped down. "You know, Olivia, I'm really glad you are here. It's been so quiet around here. You remind me of your mother when she was your age."

Olivia stared at her feet. She didn't know what to say.

"Go ahead and take a shower and use lots of soap to get any spines I might have missed," Aunt said as she left the room, leaving Olivia to ponder how to turn on a shower with no knobs and only a nasty, old showerhead hanging straight down from the ceiling.

After dinner, Olivia skimmed the index of *The Field Guide to North American Birds* that she found in the bookshelf. B . . . Bobwhite, Northern . . . *Colinus virginianus* . . . page 47. She flipped through the book to page 47. A chill went down her skin. It was a picture of the brown chicken in the woods. Olivia quickly looked around. It was dark outside the windows. The witch could be staring at her right now and she wouldn't even know. Gnat was sitting on a big overstuffed couch playing another video game. Cheeto was sprawled by the door. A huge colorful mask that Aunt said was from Bali stared over them all. It seemed so quiet inside. Safe. Weird, but safe.

Uncle came into the room. "Let's have a story," he announced.

"Eh –," Olivia countered. Gnat didn't move a muscle except for his fingers on the game.

"Let's have a story!" he boomed. He walked over to Gnat and lifted the headphones off his ears. "*A stor . . . y!*" Uncle would not be denied. He jumped onto the couch between them. Something down deep in the cushions snapped.

"What I'm going to tell you is completely true and I've never told another soul," he began.

4

Tesla Seeds and Wolverines

"When I was a young man, I was friends with a man named Nikola Tesla. He was a famous inventor, equally famous as Thomas Edison. You *do* know who Edison is right?"

Gnat stared blankly at him and grinned.

"You know, the inventor . . . ?" he asked again.

Gnat grinned.

"Just ignore him," Olivia warned.

"Well, anyway, Nikola and Edison were rivals. Every time I turned around, they were both inventing something new and amazing. Edison invented the light bulb. Nikola invented the radio. Edison invented the phonograph, Nikola invented the AC motor. And on and on they went. They both wanted to be the greatest inventor to ever live. But more than anything, Nikola wanted to harness the power of the Earth and provide free energy to the world. He realized electricity could be distributed anywhere without wires and without bills from the electric company. Imagine that, being able to turn on the light without having to plug it into the wall! He thought Edison was just trying to make money instead of making the world a better place."

"Then, one day, when I returned from a trip to India, Nikola was a changed person. He didn't want to talk to anybody. He didn't answer the door when I knocked. He had fallen into cavorting with mystics and priests from overseas. The newspapers said he was mentally ill and was obsessed with the number three. He became interested only in cosmic rays and telluric currents."

"What are tell . . . ur . . . ic currents?" Olivia asked. Gnat grinned blankly.

"Telluric currents are the invisible magnetic fields that the Earth generates. Here let me show you." Uncle walked over to a desk and rummaged through the bottom drawer.

"Ah, here it is. This compass points to the North Pole, see? Well, it turns out that it doesn't really point to the North Pole, it points to the *magnetic* North Pole. The magnetic pole is the point of strongest magnetic output from the planet. The thing is, the magnetic pole moves. It isn't a single place. It isn't a place at all actually. It is an outpouring of telluric energy. The *magnetic* field around the Earth is a three-dimensional field, like a bird cage around the planet, only it never stops moving and fluctuating. The *telluric* field is that same birdcage flowing through the planet itself, underground and such. Energy flows out of the Earth at the magnetic poles, but it must return to the Earth. What goes up must come down, right?"

"A compass is only capable of reacting in two-dimensions, it isn't an accurate representation of the magnetic field. You see?" He showed Olivia the needle spinning. "It only sees in straight lines. It can point you toward the magnetic pole, but it doesn't show you the magnetic currents and waves fluctuating all around us. It doesn't show you where the energy reenters the planet. It is like being in a submarine and only having a tiny window to see through. Everything you see is true, but it is only a very small piece of the whole picture."

Olivia had a worried look on her face and raised one eyebrow. She was afraid to ask what cosmic rays were. She assumed they came from outer space.

"I'm sorry. I get excited. It will all become clear. Many months passed and Nikola wouldn't see anybody. I left messages for him and nope, not a peep. Then, one day, I was shopping at the used bookstore, and I picked up an old book on the burning of ancient Alexandria's Library. A tattered note fell out from between the pages. It read:

Meet me under the 2nd Street bridge, Eastside. 4 P. M. Nikola."

"Who was this note for? How did Nikola know I would possibly find it? He had no reason to believe that I would be looking at that particular book on that particular day. I was filled with doubt and questions. It might not even have been *my* friend Nikola. Maybe it was a note left decades ago by another Nikola. But I did what it asked. And just as promised, at 4:00 p.m., Nikola was there. He stood in the shadow of the bridge and talked quietly. He looked exhausted and dirty.

"Nikola told me that he was being watched and followed, and warned me to be very careful. He needed me to do something very important for him and he would pay me all of the fortune that he had earned inventing over the years. He handed me two wooden boxes the size of shoe boxes, one marked 'N,' one marked 'S.' Nikola whispered, 'These are the seeds. I need you to place the N at the Magnetic North Pole and the S at the Magnetic South Pole. Whatever you do, do NOT open either box until you are at the pole and ready to plant it. Also, you must go alone.'"

"I told him that this was a big job and would take me a year to complete. You don't go wandering around the poles on a whim, you know.

Especially alone. He then handed me an envelope with his entire life's fortune. "I'm counting on you," he said. "I am too tired and they are watching me."

"What is this about? You are asking me to risk my life," I asked.

Nikola's eyes darted back and forth. He leaned in close to my ear, "There is a third pole, Harold. And it explains *everything*. They will kill you for it."

"I wasn't sure what he meant at the time, but for some reason, I believed him. Back then, it was my job to lead expeditions. I was used to actually helping someone *else* get to an exotic place. Certainly I could do it alone. It might even be easier because I wouldn't have to haul some bookworm scientist on my back up a mountain or across a river of piranhas."

"OK, Gnat. You are going to have to stop grinning at me like that. I haven't even seen you blink in the last ten minutes," Uncle put his hand on Gnat, who promptly fell over onto his side, fast asleep.

"Well, I'll be. Maybe we should continue this tomorrow."

"You can finish. There isn't anything to watch on our invisible TV," Olivia said.

"All right," Uncle chuckled. "So I made my way north with the box marked 'N.' It was very heavy for its size. It was almost impossible for me to keep the box closed as I couldn't wait to see what was inside. I traveled as far as I could by train. Then I traveled as far as I could by ship. Finally, I had to buy twelve dogs and a sled. I loaded up that sled with all of the salt pork that could fit, a gun, snowshoes, skis, and plenty of blankets. I went during winter because I knew it would be easier to travel on snow than traveling on summer mud.

During the winter, the sun doesn't even rise in the Arctic, you know. It stays dark twenty-four hours a day. The dogs and I traveled by the light of the aurora borealis, the northern lights. Wow, what a trip! All of those beautiful colors swirling in the sky! Here is a little secret, Olivia, that no one in the world knows, not even your aunt. Sometimes, when the dogs were asleep and the wind silent, I could *hear* the northern lights. Whizzing and whirling in the sky like giant ghosts. Swooshing and buzzing. I never told anyone because I knew no one would believe me.

"I believe you!" Olivia piped in.

Uncle put his hand on her head. "Thank you," he said, "you are very kind."

"The traveling was getting harder and harder," he continued. "I crossed over glaciers and fjords. I saw an old wooden ship trapped in the ice, the sails still flapping on the masts. The weather became unbearable and I was running out of salt pork. The dogs were getting worn out and they stopped wanting to run. I could hear wolves and began to fear that a polar bear was stalking us. Wolverines were always circling around, just far enough away that I couldn't shoot them.

Then, on the northern edge of Baffin Island, just west of Clyde River, I found a small Inuit town. Those nice people took me in and fed me. But it was clear that the dogs were not going to run for me anymore. They were exhausted. My only option was to walk myself to the North Pole."

"Then I had an idea. A crazy idea. I don't know if the cold finally got into my brain, or if the aurora made me lose my senses. I had a rope that was a quarter mile long, so I fashioned a harness trap. Inside the trap I put what was left of the pork. I put my skis and backpack on. And then I waited. And waited. Snow drifted and piled up on me. The villagers came out to me and put their hands on me to see if I was still alive. And then it happened. A wolverine came to the bait. I sprung the trap. Perfect! I had harnessed a wolverine! And off we went, three times faster than the dogs. What you may not know about wolverines is how strong and fast they are. They can run twenty-four-hours-a-day for two weeks. I skied along a quarter mile behind him, like a water-skier. I had rigged the harness so I could steer the wolverine in the direction that I wanted to go, but when I pulled out my compass it was as if he already knew what to do. He ran for two days pulling me and I never had to change his direction. We crossed two hundred miles of ice and snow, lit only by the green and blue aurora."

"And then he just stopped. He sat down on his haunches and stared at me. Even that far away, I could see his yellow eyes glowing in the Arctic darkness. We were there. The Magnetic North Pole! The thing is, it didn't look like anything. There weren't any lights or signs. Only miles and miles of ice. But I could sure *feel* something. I was energized, invigorated. I forgot my hunger and exhaustion. I took out the N box and carefully undid the latch. I finally would be able to see what the seed looked like. Inside was a perfectly round, dark silver ball. As the lid came up, the ball *jumped!* Now I was convinced I was crazy. I lifted it out and placed it on the snow. The seed rose up from the ground and hovered a few inches up in the air. It was moving on its own! I had never seen anything like it. It shot to the left twenty feet, adjusted its position, and settled just barely above the snow. The seed had found the right place for itself! To the seed, the earth's magnetic currents were as obvious as a river and it wanted to be directly in the flow. Remember how I told you that the magnetic pole moves? Well, the seed moves with it, like a sailor adjusts to the wind. It was Tesla's greatest invention and nobody knows about it to this day. Except me.

And now you. It is still there to this day, following the magnetic currents across the vast tundra."

"I had done it!"

"My wolverine stood up, trotted along the rope right past my feet, and started running south. Two days later we were back in the Inuit village. The winter turned rough and I had to spend the rest of the season on Baffin Island. Let's just say that I've eaten my share of seal meat. I was also way behind schedule. Back in the US, I didn't even try to communicate with Nikola. He didn't want anyone to know what I was doing."

"It is getting late. I will tell you about my trip to the South Pole another night. But suffice it to say that I was successful, even if it did take me twice as long. Part of my finger is still down there somewhere I suppose." Uncle held his hand up and showed Olivia the stub where his right ring finger used to be.

"Gross," Olivia could barely peek at the stump.

"When I got back from the South Pole, I learned that Nikola had died mysteriously of a heart attack and the government had seized all of his research papers and inventions. There was nothing left. Just an empty room. I called his laboratory in Colorado and no one answered. The American public thought he was a crazy old man, and the government made sure that was the way it stayed. I knew there was more to what was going on. What was Nikola up to? How could they ruin a man like that and take everything? I called every government office and no one knew anything. I was rich with Nikola's fortune and didn't even know why. I'm telling you, they murdered him! They murdered him!"   Uncle's voice was getting louder. His tiny eyes grew large and wild.

"They killed him for what he knew!"

In a flash of gingham and freckles, Aunt came rushing into the room and tackled Uncle from his chair to the floor. "Don't you upset the kids with your crazy schemes," Aunt screamed as she pinned his arms back. "Let's get everyone into bed. Come on. *Right now!*" Aunt scooped up Gnat and hustled off to the far-reaches of the house.

Olivia stood up to go to bed. Uncle picked himself off the floor, grabbed her by the arm and said quietly and quickly, "Olivia. A package arrived six months after I returned. Inside was a measuring tool, a meter of sorts. I call it the Teslatron. I still have it. I realized the seeds were injecting particles into the telluric currents and now I can follow them with the Teslatron. Now I could figure out how it all works. The third pole is somewhere around here. The third pole is where all of the energy flowing from the magnetic poles reenters the Earth. Its discovery will change everything. And it is out here. In these woods!"

Olivia pulled her arm away and walked to her bedroom. "There is no TV, and I'm forced to live in a madhouse," she thought. What does she care about a third pole? There is no way Uncle is that old. But she fell asleep dreaming about fierce freckles, packages with no senders, the northern lights humming in their own beauty above her in the sky, and a wild wolverine pulling her deeper and deeper into darkness.

5

You Are Early

Something was moving. A faint squeak. A flutter in the air. A trembling on the floor. It was late. The moon glowed silver into her bedroom. Olivia startled awake and looked up at the window. Tree frogs were hunting in the condensation on the glass. Their limber shadows leapt and stretched on the floor surrounding her enormous bed. There! Again, something rustled in the air. Olivia panicked. Was the Bobwhite Witch outside her window right now, trying to break in? Were the corals emerging from beneath the house, flowing like ribbons under her bed?

Her door slowly opened, creaking on its antique iron hinges. A tiny hand curled around the doorframe. Olivia's heart stopped. Gnat waddled into her room. Without a word, he stumbled toward her bed and climbed in next to her. He sniffled like he had been crying. His skin was hot and moist. He curled up and soon, he was sleeping again.

Outside, the air conditioner sputtered to life. She could feel it rumbling through the walls. Gnat snored quietly as he unconsciously gathered all of the pillows into his arms. Olivia stared at the frogs on the glass. She watched one's throat bubble up into a croak.

Tsk tsk tsk.

Shhhh shhhhh shhh.

A plump green frog walked slowly through the dew. A little drop of water ran down the glass wherever he stepped. Carefully, he walked and hopped along the window as though a speck of glue grew from each of his toes. Olivia slipped out of bed and crept closer to the window. Her nose was barely an inch away from the frog as he worked methodically across the glass. Olivia thought he was cute with his bulging gold eyes, yellow stripes, and round toes. The moon shone so brightly on the white sands of the yard and woods that it reminded her of deep Wisconsin snow. The dwarf woods looked more alive and magical than ever before.

More frogs crossed over the green frog's trail, adding their own tracks. Their trails crossed each other and crossed again, creating an intricate intersection of lines and dots. A thin cloud must have moved over the moon, because suddenly the frog tracks looked so much different to Olivia. The changing light made it obvious. The frog tracks were words! They looked like this:

$$أنت مبكّرة$$

The language looked familiar. She ran over to the nightstand and found a small pad of paper and copied it down. The strange curls and lines were hard to get right, especially in the dark. She crumpled up and tossed several pages before she got it just the way she wanted it. She remembered where she had seen these words before. A few years ago, her Mom had sent her paper money from Iraq. The frog-words were the same kind of writing that was printed so finely on those colorful bills. Maybe her Mom was sending her a message the only way she knew how! Maybe Dad didn't give her their new phone number and she was contacting her through the great international network of amphibians!

The green frogs leapt out into the bushes, leaving only their silver sentence glowing on the glass. For frogs, this short phrase was the ultimate achievement in the literary arts. Olivia knew no one would ever believe her, but no one would believe many of the things that had happened to her this past day. She looked over at Gnat. He had flipped over on his back and sprawled his arms over the edge of the bed. She grabbed her pad of paper and walked toward the living room.

The Milligan house was much weirder in the dark. Sand scorpions ruled the house at night and only by walking bravely, without any hint of fear, could they be shamed into not biting her tender bare feet. A wooden Bakuba statue stuck with hundreds of rusty iron nails reached out as she passed, trying to snag her nightgown with its points. Tiny Tibetan bells twinkled. A jade dragon scurried under the cabinet, hunting roaches. An Algonquin doll made of porcupine quills stared at her as she walked past. In the library, each nodule of opal trapped in Uncle's boulder caught the moonlight and burned like rainbows in the darkness. She flipped on the light and everything returned to its rightful place on the shelves. The clock mechanism clicked into place and a satisfying gong indicated that it was 3:30 a.m..

Olivia looked up at the enormous bookshelves towering over her. There were thousands of books, and she was pretty sure there wouldn't be one that could translate frog-words. There were books on anatomy, books on art, books on myths, books on botany and biology. Books on butterflies by Nabokov. Books on fantastic dreams by Jung and Brohm. Poetry books poured off the top shelf. A book on hyperbolic polytopes begged to be picked up and browsed. There was a whole section on Tesla. Thousands of little paper notes stuck out from the pages. She scanned the shelves for books on Florida and pulled out a book called *Amphibians of the Subtropics.* It didn't say anything about frogs writing sentences, or salamanders for that matter, although she couldn't resist reading a few pages about amphiuma who sleep under dry lake beds for years at a time before emerging in the hurricane floods.

She found a bookshelf dedicated to mysterious foreign lands. There, stuck between a book on ancient Japanese sword-making and Viking funereal ships, was a tiny beautiful book. It was covered with embossed gold scrollwork and medallions of lapis blue, but it didn't have a title on the binding. She pulled the tiny book off the shelf. On the inside cover, in fancy script, it said *Learn Arabic.*

Olivia stepped down from the stool and started flipping through the frail, thin pages. Her mind raced. Nothing made sense. Each Arabic letter lined up with its English equal, but she could not figure out what the frog was saying. Then she remembered how her Mom had told her that they write backwards in Iraq, from right to left. Suddenly, the sentence started to come together. And then . . . there it was. Her pencil fell from her fingers and clattered on the wood floor. The message from the Arabic frogs, the one that no person in the world would believe was written in the dew on her bedroom window, was

YOU ARE EARLY.

6

The Tortoise Burrow

"You are early," Olivia thought, awaking with a jump. "Early for what?" The sun poured through the window with all of its heart, burning away whatever was left of the dewy frog-words. Gnat had left her room sometime earlier in the morning. Olivia tucked *Learn Arabic* under her pillow and jumped to the floor. It was 9:30 and she was supposed to meet Doug at Mr. Gruffle's in half an hour!

She remembered a rule of the house that Aunt told her yesterday: *Always look inside your shoes first.* Olivia didn't know what she was supposed to be looking for as she peered deep into her dark musty sneakers. "Crazy coot," she muttered.

She wolfed down a bowl of Honeycombs and rushed outside. There was no sign of the green frog on her bedroom window. In fact, there was no sign of any frog at all. It was if the moon made frogs every night and sun destroyed them every day.

She looked down at the coral snake highway. The snakes had already left on their mysterious errands for the day. In the exact spot where she had left a pile of blueberries yesterday, lay three oblong beads the size of raspberries. One black, one red, and one yellow. They blazed like little suns on the white sand. She carefully picked each one up. When she held them to the light, they sparkled with every color of the rainbow. The deeper she stared into them, the more she saw swirling inside.

"Uncle! Uncle!" she ran inside. "The corals left me some beads!"

"Huh? What is this?" he said, looking up from his newspaper. "You say the snakes gave you these?"

"I left them some blueberries yesterday, and this is what they left for me in return," she shouted.

"Well I doubt that. Coral snakes do not eat blueberries and they certainly do not have any beads," he said sharply and returned to his paper. "They probably fell out of your aunt's craft chest. Don't be silly."

But Olivia knew that it was true as she strung them onto a cord and tied it around her neck. She made sure that the yellow bead was in between the red and the black beads because that was exactly how the bands of color were on the snakes themselves. Black, yellow, red, yellow, black, yellow, red, and so on.

She thought it would best to keep quiet about the Arabic frog's words from last night. If he didn't believe her about the snakes, he certainly wasn't going to believe that a frog was writing sentences on her window. How could a man who builds churches for walkingsticks and was once pulled across the Arctic by a wolverine not see the truth? She believed *his* silly story.

"I'm going to meet Doug. We are going to flag tortoise holes," she shouted, slamming the phone down after leaving another message for Dad. But just as she reached for the back door, Gnat appeared, fully dressed with small boots, a backpack, a matching hat, and plenty of sunscreen on his face.

"Out of batteries," he said.

"Why don't you take your brother with you?" Aunt suggested in a tone reminiscent of an order.

"He will slow us down. We have a lot of tortoises to find."

"Your brother really needs some sun. He already has some water in his backpack. And I made some snacks. He has been talking about this all morning."

"Aaargh. All right, Gnat. But if you slow us down, I'm leaving you out there," she said grabbing his hand.

"Olivia!" Aunt scolded. But it was too late, they were already halfway across the yard with Cheeto following close behind.

"This," Olivia announced by the back fence, "is the walkingstick church. Inside, the brave and noble walkingsticks hold their exclusive conventions."

"What do they talk about?" Gnat asked.

"Oh, they don't talk. They are the only known nation to communicate only by smell. It is a beautiful language. Come close, and sniff."

Gnat leaned in close to the church entrance and took a deep breath through his nose.

"Aaaaaaaaaaah Choooooo!" he sneezed.

"Come on," Olivia ordered with a crooked smile. Knowing nothing of sibling tricks and sarcasm, the walkingsticks heard Olivia's kind words and swelled with pride.

The kids plunged deeper and deeper into the scrub. Soon, Cheeto stopped following as he smelled many interesting things that needed investigation.

As they rushed along the sandy pathways, she remembered Doug saying there were bears and panthers out here. It didn't make sense how such big animals could live in all this sand.

Olivia's mind raced over the desert stories she had read last night as she sat up hoping for more frog messages. The desolate sands of Libya, the slipsands of Cufra that pulled unwary travelers down like waterless quicksand, the entire desert armies that laid in wait under the dunes for an ambush, the seifs and barchans slowly marching for centuries, the jinniyah spirits of fire, hibernating sand dragons, lost tombs, the child-prince of Persia. She couldn't remember the details of the stories, but they hung in her mind like foggy dreams.

Gnat stumbled along behind her, huffing and puffing. He was sweating profusely and kept wiping his forehead under his cap. It was more exercise than he'd ever had. He certainly was outfitted with enough heavy equipment and supplies to handle any tortoise burrow flagging emergency. Olivia walked faster.

"See, Gnat. This is the Vomiting Holly," she said, brushing past the unassuming tree.

"Cooool. Does . . . it . . . really . . . throw up?" he asked breathing heavily.

"Uh, well, no, dummy. The tree doesn't throw up. It makes *you* throw up if you eat it."

"Hmmm," Gnat eyed the tree suspiciously, obviously disappointed.

"Why don't you try some?" she snickered.

Her footsteps pressed hard into the sand. For half an hour she trudged ahead. Somehow, Gnat was keeping up behind her.

"You are late," Doug said, stepping out from behind some dwarf oak trees.

"No, I'm early," Olivia shot back.

"I have ten-fifteen." Doug looked at his watch.

"Forget it," she snipped. "I'm late."

"Who's the shrimp?" Doug asked.

"I'm Gnat, Power Soldier Level Six."

"Eh. OK. Well, be careful," Doug warned. "I've been finding traps like this all over the place."

Next to Mr. Gruffle's burrow, a young tree had been bent over and a rope was looped around on the ground. A small stick had been jammed into the sand and the rope was knotted around it. A crumpled up piece of aluminum foil was attached to the top of the stick.

"This has to be the Mutch twins. They must think the aluminum will attract the witch."

"Witch?" Gnat exclaimed. "Where's the witch?"

"It's just a story," Doug comforted him.

Olivia walked over to the trap and gave the rope a tug. The trigger stick fell over. The trap sprung, but the tree never snapped upright. It was permanently bent over. "Some trap. This hunk of junk couldn't catch anything."

"Yeah! What a hunk of junk," Gnat repeated, examining the contraption with authority.

"You should have seen the box trap they had over there," Doug said, removing two objects from his pockets.

"What do you have there?" Olivia asked.

"Walkie-talkies. I brought them so we can talk to each other. I mean, if you want."

"These aren't just any walkie-talkies," Olivia said as she turned one over in her hand. "These are Aquaman walkie-talkies."

"Um . . . yeah," Doug looked embarrassed.

"What? The store ran out of Batman walkie-talkies?" she said with a fake tone of panic.

"Well, they were on sale."

"Maybe we can call some dolphins. Or a trout."

"Cool!" Gnat grabbed it out of Olivia's hands and started to turn the knobs. "Hello. Hello. Come in, Bravo Team."

"Like this." Doug leaned over and adjusted the power switch. "Hold down this button to talk."

"Hello." Gnat's voice crackled through Doug's walkie-talkie. "Hello."

"Conserve your batteries," Doug responded. Gnat must have remembered what happened to his video game because he immediately turned off the walkie-talkie and clipped it to his belt.

Doug looked over to Olivia. She was on her hands and knees face down again at the opening to Mr. Gruffle's burrow. The old tortoise bravely crawled up his burrow within inches of Olivia's face. She could feel his breath huffing against her cheek. His large gray head silently nodded up and down.

"Whoa," Doug whispered. "I've never seen one do that."

He could hear Olivia talking to the tortoise as if they could understand each other.

"Did you sleep well last night Mr. Gruffle? . . . I didn't. Yes, they are new. The corals gave them to me."

Doug looked at Gnat. "Is she always like this?"

Gnat shrugged. "Are there bears?" he asked, spinning around expecting to see one.

"Oh yeah. They are all over the place. Here, look," Doug said, pointing to a big track in the sand. Gnat placed his hand in the wide track.

"Whoa. That's big."

"Yeah, but you never see them 'cept at night when they come out of the woods to get into garbage cans. They love garbage." Doug turned back toward the tortoise hole.

"Hey, I want to show you guys something," he called out. He heard Olivia tell Mr. Gruffle goodbye as she walked over.

"What is it?" she asked.

"It's this way a little bit," he answered. As they walked, Gnat scooted ahead until he found something that interested him: big ant colonies, banana spiders, bear tracks.

"He's just like a puppy," Olivia joked.

It was a hot day. Really hot. The sand under their feet seemed to be even hotter than the sun. It burned up through the bottoms of their shoes. "Is it always this hot?" Olivia asked, pulling at her sweat-soaked clothes.

"Pretty much," Doug said, "it only cools off in winter. A little."

"It's like a desert out here," she complained.

"Did your Dad call you back?"

"No, not yet. I left him another message this morning. I wish I knew what was going on."

"What do you mean?"

"I mean he just sent us off. Mom is in the war and he just sent us off for no reason."

"What's it like anyway? Snow, I mean," Doug asked, looking down at the ground.

"It's a pain. But it's fun too. Skating, sledding, snow forts, icicles."

"Really? And you don't go to the beach ever?"

"I've been to Lake Michigan a bunch of times. And once we camped on an island in Lake Superior. That's kind of like going to the ocean. But they freeze in the winter. And there aren't crabs and stuff. So, do you surf and hula dance?"

Doug blushed. "I think you mean Hawaii. Some people around here surf though. There isn't much to do around here."

"There's not much to do in Sun Prairie either," Olivia countered.

Olivia felt like something was following them. She kept turning her head and straining her ears, listening for footsteps or breaking twigs. Plenty of old, dry leaves littered the ground. Whatever was following them was very careful about where it stepped.

Doug pulled off old acorns from the dwarf oaks and chucked them as far as he could. He seemed completely oblivious to the panther or witch that was behind them. Gnat saw Doug hit a pine tree with an acorn and suddenly became interested in the game. The first acorn Gnat threw bounced right off the back of Doug's head.

"Hey!" Doug yelped. Gnat laughed as he awkwardly threw a whole handful of acorns and ran off ahead on the trail. "Bonus points! Bonus points!" he yelled triumphantly.

Olivia whispered to Doug, "You go around that way." They both scampered off on either side of the main trail, running to cut Gnat off and barrage him with fistfuls of acorns. She could hear him giggling up ahead. She ran as quietly as she could, making sure not to step on any sticks. She must have been good at it, because she could hear Doug crashing through the bushes like a buffalo. She saw Gnat in a clearing with his back to her. He was looking up. When she snuck closer, she realized what he was looking at. The trees seemed to suddenly grow enormous. Palms towered in the sky. Big green oaks and tupelos soared upward. The tiny scrub forest behind them looked like brush in comparison. Sheets of hanging moss twisted in the breeze. The air grew cooler. She closed her eyes and listened. There were birds singing everywhere.

"Ah Ya!" Doug screamed as he launched twenty acorns towards Gnat. Gnat hit the ground and covered his head as they pelted around him. Laughing, he said, "You got me. For that you shall pay."

Doug paused, surprised at the way Gnat talked. "So be it! The Acorn War has begun!"

"What is this place?" Olivia asked as she stepped out of the bushes.

"Come on, I'll show you," Doug said, walking past the enormous tree trunks and stepping carefully over the maze of roots.

"These trees must be thousands of years old," Olivia said. "Maybe we can build a treehouse up there."

"This is where the bears have parties," Gnat proclaimed.

Doug stopped and examined every spider web, hopeful that a previously undiscovered species of spider patiently waited for him. He put a check mark on his clipboard every time he found an insect or saw a bird flittering in the treetops.

The trail worked its way downward. The green shade felt good on Olivia's skin. The singing birds didn't seem to mind that three children were chattering amongst them. Olivia turned and looked behind her. They had descended further than she realized. It was another world from the hot, sandy scrub.

And then she saw what was at the end of the trail. Up over a little rise and beyond a thick stand of palm trees, glowing and sparkling with all the light of the sun, a bright spring flowed from the ground. It was the prettiest blue color Olivia had ever seen, prettier than the sky. Large white birds stood around the spring, staring into its depths. She couldn't turn away, it was so beautiful. Olivia had never seen anything like this in Wisconsin, where the waters were dark from the tamarack trees and filled with mud and algae. The spring was the most refreshing thing she had ever seen, like it was created just for her. Nothing would stop her from swimming in it. She started taking off her shoes to jump in.

"Wait!" Doug warned. "Check for gators first. And snakes." He picked up a rock from the shoreline and clunked it into the middle of the spring. The white birds took off squawking angrily. He watched for a moment. Olivia hadn't even thought about alligators. The ripples from the rock circled out and dissipated in the shallow weeds.

"OK, it's safe," he said, splashing into the spring.

An old palm tree hung out over the water. Olivia worked her way out along the trunk. Her toes clung to the rough bark. The spring below her was so clear she could see tiny fish swimming along in the deep weeds. Most of the spring bottom consisted of bright white limestone and it seemed to enhance the sparkling waters. She looked over at Gnat, who had taken his shoes off and was swinging a stick at a giant yellow butterfly.

She jumped.

In a flash, the cold water stunned her skin and knocked the breath from her lungs. Her screams echoed in the woods around them. Doug laughed. She could feel the fresh, clean water rushing up around her from underground. She felt weightless and invincible. Paddling out into the middle, she noticed that she swam faster than she ever had before. It was easy. With one kick she skimmed across the surface. She felt like she could swim for hours and never get tired. Without realizing it, Olivia was smiling and laughing. She turned over onto her back and floated.

Up in the sky, a swallow-tailed kite soared. It sliced through the air with the gentlest of efforts, swooping and lilting. Its bold black and white feathers stood in stark contrast against the blue atmosphere. Olivia could tell — she didn't know how — that it was a girl. She flew with such joy, such contentment. Olivia watched every tiny feather reach out to the air and embrace the world.

The kite seemed reluctant to fly beyond the borders of the spring. She descended closer to the water, her forked tail tilting tighter into the faint breeze. More than just a bird, she emanated light. Faster she spun. Her tail grew longer, blurred. Her wings extended, growing faint, like a smile growing beyond the limits of its face. Olivia could see the sky *through* her body. She dissipated, becoming air . . . faster . . . whirling. She became more and more air, until finally she flew level with the water straight at Olivia only a few feet away . . . and faded into . . . nothing. The slightest melody rippled along the water and breezed through Olivia's hair, tossing her curls.

Olivia looked around. The boys were taking turns shoving each other from the palm tree. They hadn't noticed the kite at all. She knew the disappearing bird was an odd thing to see, but it actually seemed normal enough. It wasn't scary, more like the natural conclusion of complete happiness. That was how Olivia felt in the water. She wanted to be a water kite. She rolled backwards into a somersault. She skipped across the spring like a dolphin.

Pushing the hair from her face, her finger caught a gnarl. She shoved her fingers harder to loosen the tangle. With a distinctive click, she felt her birthday barrette unlatch and fall. With one quick gulp of air Olivia dove. She saw the red barrette drop down toward the cave opening. Olivia kicked harder trying to catch it. She could see the little bejeweled bumblebee glittering in the light as it wobbled down. The bubbles from her hands plunging down shimmied silver up to the surface. Fish darted in front of her face. She forgot about the witch. She forgot about Dad. She forgot where she was, or when. All she wanted was to catch the barrette. Deeper and deeper she reached for the falling barrette, until finally it fell beyond any hope into the spring's heart, its source.

And then, as from a foggy distant dream, she heard faint voices, "Come on! Come on! Over here!" Were the turtles calling her? Did she suddenly understand the language of the fishes? She spun around. A school of bream glittered by. The great cavernous spring opened up beneath her, like a mouth yawning her inward. "Come on, Olivia!"

She kicked up to the surface.

"Over here!" Gnat and Doug were yelling and waving their hands at her. A flood of memories rushed back to her. With a flick of her legs she propelled over to the boys.

"Alligator!" they shouted pointing to the middle of the spring. Gnat threw his stick as hard as he could.

Olivia jumped from the water and looked back. An enormous alligator cruised slowly along the surface. Its dark head split through the water with terrible ease. It had bumpy, black, leathery skin. It looked like it could swallow a car. Even from this far away, she could see its sharp white teeth gleaming in the sun.

"It swam right over you," Doug screamed. "Weren't you paying attention?" A chill ran down Olivia's skin. She reached for her neck.

"He could have eaten you, Olivia," Gnat squealed. She looked down. His feet were bleeding from stepping on sharp rocks.

"Whatever." She rolled her eyes. But inside, she couldn't figure out how the alligator didn't notice her. Why hadn't it attacked?

"Why didn't you see it? What were you thinking? You were under water *forever*." Doug's voice was getting higher and higher.

"Just shut up and leave me alone! *Shut up!*" Olivia screamed and ran up the trail leaving the two boys to stand there and gawk at each other. Why can't they just relax and leave her alone? Nothing bad happened. No one got hurt. Who cares anyway?

She sat down on a big root with a thump. Her mind was swirling. Dizzied images and feelings she couldn't even start to put words to spun out of control, skipped and whirled, and none of it made any sense. This whole thing was just plain stupid. Flagging stupid tortoise burrows. Frogs that write Arabic words that don't mean anything. Stupid bobwhites. Stupid snakes with beads. This must be a dream. She had lost the red barrette, and now she was caught in a nightmare. If she closed her eyes tight enough and opened them again, maybe she would be at home sitting underneath the cottonwood tree with a herd of gentle deer instead of in this sweaty backwoods swamp filled with alligators and poisonous snakes. And who cares if Dad ever calls or comes to get her? He is a jerk anyway. He didn't have time for her. Mom is going to come home soon and they can start a quiet life somewhere like Colorado or Japan.

And then she realized how hard she was crying. Sobbing, really. Tears were not just coming from her eyes. Tears were coming from all over her body, from places she didn't know existed. Her toes donated tears. The tiny spaces between the puzzle-bones of her ankles donated tears. Tears squeezed like lemons from her elbows. Her skin tingled with them. Her lungs heaved. Her scalp vibrated. Her whole head lurched and burned.

Tears rushed and flowed up and out of her like an unstoppable salty spring. And for a moment, that spring of tears was the perfect place for her to swim. More perfect even than the wild blue water she had just emerged from.

Ten minutes later, they were all walking quietly back to the Milligan house. The boys were afraid to say anything. They strolled along, occasionally chucking acorns at each other. Every time Olivia glanced their way, they would pretend to study a flower or a bug. She knew they were joking around behind her. She heard them snickering and punching each other. Snap! A branch cracked behind her.

She whipped around, "Would you two . . . " Her voice trailed off as she stared at the trail behind them.

"Would we what?" Doug asked.

"Yeah, what?" Gnat mimicked.

"Um. Ummmm," she stammered. She raised her hand slowly, pointing. The boys turned around. There, standing only twenty feet away, stood a huge black bear. He must have weighed over five hundred pounds. A thick scar ran down his cheek. He had a tuft of cinnamon red hair on his forehead and his chest was emblazoned with a white patch in the shape of a V. But the kids weren't looking at his chest. They were staring at his huge clawed feet and his enormous head. They could hear the breath rush past his nostrils.

"Grrrrwumph," the bear woofed as he sat down on his haunches.

"BEAR!" Doug screamed as he flew past Olivia. She reached back and grabbed Gnat by the arm and ran after Doug. They sprinted as hard as they could along the narrow path. They could hear the big bear huffing and crashing through the brush behind them. Gnat's backpack was bouncing and jostling. As Doug pushed through a branch, it snapped back at Olivia's face and she fell to the ground to avoid it.

"Hey, watch out!" she yelled. The bear was right behind her, sitting again.He tilted his head to the side. Olivia scrambled to her feet and took off again.

As she ran after Doug into a sandy clearing, he suddenly disappeared. Completely disappeared. Vanished! Before she could stop running, she felt the ground beneath her feet give way. She looked up and saw Gnat enter the clearing behind her. In a split second, the sand swallowed over her head and she sank into darkness. Instinctively, she held her breath as the sand shifted loosely around her. She was falling, falling through a tortoise burrow. And then she realized that she was going to die. This was it. The end. She would have to breathe soon. Her lungs burned for air as the sand poured around her. A thought flashed through her mind. This was just like the slipsand she read about in the desert books. There is no escape. No one would ever find her just like they never found those camel caravans in Cufra who disappeared into the dunes. And she started to scream. The noise of her screaming went nowhere in the sand. Then she suddenly emerged into empty air. Her screams echoed as she fell and landed with a soft thud in the underground darkness. Olivia looked up in the dim light. A few seconds later, Gnat tumbled down after her. Doug was a few feet away wiping sand from his hair. They were at the bottom of a deep cave. The ceiling they fell from soared high above them. Olivia had sand in her ears, sand in her nose, and sand in her mouth. Gnat shook like a dog. They all looked up half-expecting the bear to come crashing down on top of them.

"Where . . . where are we?" Doug was starting to hyperventilate, and tears pooled in his eyes. "Where are we? What are we going to do?"

Gnat had skinned his knee in the fall and was on the ground moaning. Olivia started to say "I don't know." She *wanted* to say "I don't know." But truthfully, she was caught off-guard. She couldn't remember the last time anyone even asked her what she wanted or what her opinion was. And she was sure no one had actually depended on her for advice or help. Both Doug and Gnat were now crying and scared. A hot rush overcame her. She knew all three of them were now depending on her decisions. They were in trouble. Big trouble. No one knew where they were. Aunt and Uncle would search for them but only find their footsteps ending at the tortoise burrow above. Doug was her age, but he suddenly seemed very much like a young child. It was up to her to find their way out.

She remembered Dad taking her out into the woody edges of cornfields in November during deer season. He showed her how their crunchy footsteps in the white frost marked a path home as clearly as any sign or map. He taught her how to be quiet, how to look carefully at the trees, and that your imagination was your biggest enemy in the woods. They would sit up in a tree-stand under a big wool blanket, whispering about anything and everything. The deer would carefully step out below them, like slender ballerinas. Every time, Dad would always whisper, "Those are too small" or "Those are too gamey," and they would drink cocoa from a thermos. Dad was different out there. He never talked to her that way at home. That seemed like a lifetime ago. It had been years since they went deer hunting together.

Olivia took a long, slow breath. She looked Doug right in the eyes, not just at his face, but deep into his eyes with a fierceness that she didn't even know was inside her, and said, "Wow! This place is incredible!"

Doug gawked at her.

"This place is amaaaaazing!" she repeated. Doug sniffed and stood up. Gnat turned his head. In fact, they had landed on an enormous pile of shockingly white sand. As their eyes adjusted to the darkness, the details around them started to emerge. Rays of blue light streamed down from cracks in the ceiling. The cracks must be on the bottom of springs and streams because the blue light wavered and pulsed like water. It *was* amazing. It looked to Olivia like they had fallen into a stained-glass cathedral.

The kids slid down the giant sand pile until their feet stood on the sandy ground. The cave room was so big that they couldn't see any walls. A vast, quiet lake spread out in every direction. The sand pile was on a small island in the middle of the lake. Droplets echoed as they fell into the lake from the ceiling.

"This doesn't make any sense. I've never read about this and I've read everything about Florida," Doug stammered.

"This is our own secret world! You will *never* find it in any book because words can't describe it. Gnat, you are the security guard. Doug, you are the navigator. We need to find our way back to the world of the sun." Olivia's words seemed to cheer the boys up a little. Gnat adjusted his backpack and retied his shoes. He pulled a flashlight out of the pack and clicked it on. It didn't seem to penetrate the darkness of the cave in the very least.

"Save the batteries," Doug warned. Gnat clicked the light off.

Olivia stepped slowly into the lake. It was too deep to walk into for more than a few yards. The cold water was the same temperature as the spring they were swimming in earlier. Her footsteps sent ripples spreading out into the calm water. They had no way of knowing how far the ripples traveled. The darkness was impenetrable. Darkness, blue rays,

white sand. How were they going to escape from an underground island with no boat and no light? They had no way of knowing that on the distant shore, deep in the unexplored cave, the ripples from her footsteps awakened something ancient and undisturbed for eons.

7

The Tombolo

"Let's walk around this hill and see what's on the other side," Olivia whispered. Gnat was rubbing his nose, and his eyes were as big as dinner plates. They walked slowly around the hill looking out into the great cavern. As far as they could see, blue beams of light shimmered down into the dark. There was nothing else to see.

Then, as they circled the enormous hill, they saw a long sandbar extending outward from the sand hill; a tombolo.

"Woooooah," Doug exclaimed.

Stretching like a highway into the darkness, the tombolo was the only way off the island other than swimming. Its white sand sparkled and gleamed as it stretched into the darkness.

"Where do you think it goes?" Olivia asked.

"Who knows? I don't even know where we are now."

"Maybe it doesn't go anywhere. Maybe it just goes into the water."

"I guess we don't have any choice, unless you can fly."

"Yeah, unless you can fly." Gnat giggled.

"OK, smart alecks. I guess we walk," Olivia responded.

So they started walking, leaving behind the only entrance to the cave they knew. Within a minute or two, they couldn't even see the sand mountain behind them anymore. For an hour they quietly walked along the tombolo. The cool, clear water glowed in the blue light on either side of them. Olivia slipped off her shoes. As she walked, the soft sand squished up between her toes. She waded through the water for a while. It felt good. Better than wearing sneakers anyway. And if she was going to be lost and die down here, she might as well be barefoot. Then a thought occurred to her. What if her mom was lost in the desert, just like they were lost down here? Yes! That was it! It all made sense now. Dad didn't want to scare them or make them sick with worry. Dad knew both she and Gnat wouldn't sleep knowing that Mom was in trouble. He probably marched right in to see the general and demanded to parachute behind enemy lines. Or the president himself. Or maybe the army wouldn't allow any of it and Dad had to sneak into Iraq on his own. Maybe he posed as a deckhand on that ship she saw at the beach. That is why he won't return her calls. He was probably, right now, speeding across the desert in a Jeep full of turban-wearing rebels searching for her. Yes. She could only pray that Mom wasn't injured too badly or held captive. Right then and there, Olivia vowed to never, *ever,* tell Gnat the truth. He was too young to understand what has happened. He has his hands full dealing with what kind of cereal to pick out and the lack of batteries at Aunt and Uncle's.

"I think I figured it out," Doug said. "We must be in the aquifer."

"The what?"

"Yeah, the what?" Gnat repeated.

"The aquifer," Doug said with the tone of a teacher. "Underneath Florida is a vast network of limestone caves and waterways. Rainwater drips down through the sand and lands in the aquifer. The water here might be thousands of years old. It's where our drinking water comes from."

"That's very . . . interesting. Any idea how to get out of the aquifer, Nature Boy?"

"Of course."

"Do you mind sharing with the rest of us?"

"The aquifer emerges onto the surface in the form of springs. Like the one we were swimming in earlier."

"So we just need to find a spring."

"I guess. But this isn't exactly like I read. This should be filled with water. It doesn't make any sense that we are *walking* in the aquifer."

Just then, Gnat plopped down on the sand. "I need recharging."

"Let's take a break." Olivia sat next to him.

"I guess my notes are all ruined from the dripping water." Doug threw down his clipboard. "You know, we have been walking for a while. We must be under Orlando or something. We could be underneath Disney. Well, I guess not. It takes over an hour to get there in a car. Well, maybe, because all you do is sit at traffic lights anyway. But maybe we are walking north . . . hmmmmm."

"Well, there is no need to litter!" Olivia picked up his clipboard, rolling her eyes, unzipped Gnat's backpack, and started to slide it in. "Uh . . . Gnat?"

"What?"

"Do you realize that your pack is full of snacks?"

"Of course."

"Were you planning on telling us?"

"You have snacks?" Doug suddenly stopped trying to figure out if they could be under Disney World or not. "Snacks!"

They pulled out handfuls of little fruit bars, bite-size chocolates that had melted in the sun and resolidified in the cool cave, juice drinks, and cookies. A flurry of opening wrappers and screams of joy filled the cavernous silence.

"No one gets any. I carried them. Those are mine!" Gnat yelled, reaching for a bag of potato chips that Doug had already half-finished.

"Gnat, you better hurry up or you won't get any," Olivia warned.

"You guys." Gnat was mad, but he started stuffing strawberry wafer cookies into his mouth.

"Whopper? Might anyone be interested in a Whopper?" Doug asked raising an eyebrow and doing his best British accent.

"Why, no thank you, kind sir. But perhaps you might be bothered to pass the chocolate chip cookies?" Olivia grinned.

"But of course." As he leaned over to grab the cookies, Gnat saw his chance and lunged for the Whoppers, which he wolfed down triumphantly. Maybe he won't get to eat *all* of it, but he should certainly have his choice of the treats.

"You know, that bear must not know what in the world happened. I swear he was right behind Gnat and me when we fell through."

"Yeah, I bet he is all messed up in the head wondering where his lunch went."

"He probably just wanted these snacks anyway." Gnat stopped chewing when Olivia said that.

"You were walking bear bait, Gnat!" Doug laughed. "Gimme the gummi worms."

"I'm not carrying that anymore," Gnat said pushing the pack toward Olivia.

"Well, I'm not carrying it either."

"I don't think it really matters anymore," Doug said. "It's all gone." There was only a pile of empty wrappers on the sand between them.

"Ugh. Energy cells are full." Gnat rolled onto his back.

"What . . . is . . . that?" Doug said, pointing. A white, biscuit-sized creature had emerged from the water and inched its way up the sand behind them. It looked like a spineless sea-urchin. It didn't have legs — at least it *looked* like it didn't have legs — and they couldn't see any eyes. It appeared to be hard and solid, like a smooth rock the same white color as the sand all around them. On its top, a five-pointed star was etched onto the surface of its body. The creature plowed through the sand as it moved, sometimes twisting and turning, sometimes moving straight ahead, in a manner that left doubt as to whether it actually *had* a front or back, a left or right. It moved in every direction effortlessly. It seemed curious about these strangers walking along the tombolo.

"Olivia, don't! We don't know what it is," Doug ordered. He knew all about touching things you shouldn't touch up in the woods. But it was too late. Olivia extended a finger toward the white biscuit creature. Just as the tip of her finger touched its hard, cool surface, it jumped backward with a squeak, ejecting a few drops of bright pink ink toward her. The ink soaked down into the sand.

"Whoa. Cool!" Olivia said. "Well, Nature Boy, what is it?"

"I dunno. I really don't know. He looks like a fat sand dollar but he moves too fast. Urchins only live in the ocean. Maybe he is a kind of turtle or beetle. Hmmmm . . . well that wouldn't make any sense. He doesn't have a head. He is just . . . a . . . lump. I've seen fossils that look like that. He must be some kind of echinoid."

"Echi-huh?"

"Uh, urchin. Some kind of urchin," Doug blushed.

"I think he's an alien," Gnat piped in.

"A cave urchin! We'll call him Squirt. Come here Squirt!" The cave urchin inched closer to Olivia. "Here. Have some cookie. Come on. It's all right. Cookie, yum yum!" She put the last few crumbs of cookie on the sand right in front of the Squirt. Or what she thought was his front. He plowed over the top of the crumbs and paused for a few seconds. As he moved on, they could see that the cookie crumbs had disappeared.

"He ate it!" Gnat exclaimed. "Have a gummi!" he put a candy next to Squirt who slid over and ate it just as quickly.

Olivia knelt on the sand and slowly moved her hand toward Squirt. Slowly. Slowly so he wouldn't get scared. Soon, she was stroking his back. "Awwww, how cute," she cooed.

"You better be careful," Doug warned. "That pink stuff might be poison."

"Nonsense!" Olivia quipped. "Who ever heard of pink poison?"

Squirt jumped forward toward the kids, squeaking.

"I think he wants more," Gnat said. "I'm out."

"All we have left is this yogurt raisin."

"Well, give it to him," Olivia ordered. Doug put down the raisin and leaned closer. Squirt promptly moved on top and ate it. "SQUEAK!" He hopped forward. "SQUEAK!"

"Oh, now you've done it," Olivia said.

"What? I didn't do anything," Doug snapped with a little panic in his voice.

"You fed a wild animal and now it will never leave you alone."

"You two started it, not me."

"Well, he isn't squeaking at Gnat or me."

"SQUEAK!" Squirt's hard surface shivered and flushed pale pink then back to white.

"Did you see that? He changes color too. I wonder what that means."

"He is probably mad and about to bite your finger off for not feeding him more."

"I should take him to the university and see what they say. He changes color like a cuttlefish. How peculiar."

"Don't you dare steal Squirt. He lives here." Olivia punched Doug on the shoulder as hard as she could.

"Ow! Fine! Well, I wish we had a camera."

"SQUEAK!"

"Ugh. Let's keep walking. Who knows how far we have to go to get out of here." Doug turned to go.

"Goodbye, Squirt!" Olivia chirped as she slid the backpack over her shoulders. "We will miss you!"

After a few minutes of marching along, Gnat glanced over his shoulder. "Looks like Squirt wants to come with us."

Squirt pushed through the sand like a miniature snow plow. He moved surprisingly fast and had no trouble keeping up with the kids.

"Squirt. Stay!" Olivia ordered. "Sit!"

"SQUEAK!"

"Let's just keep going. He'll get tired," Doug said.

After several more hours of walking, their legs were getting sore. They heard a distant, pounding rumble.

"What was that?" Gnat yelled out. It rumbled again.

"It sounds like a bomb," Doug offered. "I don't like it."

The water dripping from the ceiling started to quicken. Thin waterfalls trickled faster and faster, falling from high above. The whole cavern lit up with a faint flash through the ceiling cracks followed by muffled rumbling.

"It's a thunderstorm!" Olivia shouted. They walked faster hoping to find some place to get out of the dripping water. The whole Earth shook under their feet. Everywhere they looked, another waterfall gushed. Suddenly, in front of them, the lightning lit up an enormous skeleton of a wooly mammoth sticking halfway out of the water. Its long tusks arched over them as they walked past. Waterfalls tumbled and foamed all around. Another mammoth skeleton sat menacingly on the sand. Draped over the bones, as if the mammoth had only died yesterday, an elaborate suit of armor intricately fabricated from millions of small silver medallions clinked in the rain. It hung like a shining curtain over the skeleton. The armor must have weighed a ton just by itself. The long white tusks were ornamented with jewels and knives. Around each leg, a shin plate with a ring of spikes still circled the ankle bones. At the center of the head-plate, embedded into the silver, was a gleaming blue jewel.

Gnat yelled, "Come on!" as he scrambled under the enormous rib bones of the mammoth. "See? It is dry under here!"

Olivia and Doug ducked under a shoulder blade that was big enough to make a canoe out of. They sat inside the big bony chest of the mammoth and waited for the storm to end. Falling water plinked and plunked on the silver medallions overhead. It sounded like nickels in a frying pan. After all the time they had spent in the dark cave, their sense of time seemed to have dulled. Olivia felt like, since coming to Florida, she had spent more time in this cave than in the Milligans' house. She didn't know if the light coming through the ceiling was sunlight or moonlight. All she really knew was they had to find a way out of here. But for now, sitting together, dry inside the great beast and listening to the millions of raindrops dripping on their silver roof, all three soon fell asleep.

Eventually, the rumbling grew distant. The lightning dimmed.

"The storm is over," Doug announced, stretching his arms and yawning.

"Really? Oh, really?" Olivia laughed.

"I'm just saying," Doug said.

As the rain stopped dripping, they slid out between the rib bones and looked around. There were mammoth skeletons everywhere. Enormous shields and spears were littered about, like some kind of battle had been fought here thousands of years ago. Or maybe it was the glorious cemetery of the underground warrior mammoths.

"Gosh. I wonder what happened," Doug whispered, pulling a razor-sharp brassy point from the end of one of the tusks. For some reason, it didn't seem right to speak louder than a whisper in such a place.

"Guess who's here." Gnat quietly gestured down. Squirt hopped at his foot.

"SQUEAK!" Apparently Squirt didn't feel the need to be quiet here.

"Hi, Squirt. Do you know what happened here?" Olivia knelt down to pet him. "We don't have any more food. Sorry. But you can stay with us if it makes you happy."

"Seems like Squirt has friends," Doug said. Cave urchins crawled out of the water onto the sand by the hundreds. Maybe thousands. They spun and plowed and squeaked in the sand.

"See what happens when you feed wild animals?" she said, glancing sideways at him. As Olivia stepped toward the urchins, they slid out of the way like she had an invisible force field surrounding her. Gnat jumped up and the urchins all scooted back before he landed. They seemed to want to be as close as possible to their feet without getting stepped on. Several were rummaging violently through the backpack that Olivia had left on the ground.

"I hope they only eat treats," Doug whispered.

"Squirt wouldn't hurt a fly," Olivia said.

Flashes of faint color spread over the herd of urchins like disco lights. Pale green, blue, and pink rippled through their bodies like a coordinated and practiced routine.

"I think they are happy to see us."

"Or super hungry."

The urchins spread out all around them as they walked. They were quite capable of keeping up and staying just a few inches from every step.

"Which one is Squirt?" Gnat looked around.

"I dunno . . . Squirrrrrrrrrt! Squirrrrt!" Olivia called out.

"SQUEAK!" An urchin under her foot hopped.

"There he is! Hi, Squirt! Hey, he knows his name."

"You know, I've found fossils of sea urchins in the streams around here," Doug said. "There are several species of echinoids. Maybe even hundreds. All of Florida was under the ocean once and the bedrock was formed by the billions of shells and urchins. Maybe these were just left behind. Wow! We are going to be famous. I'm not talking nerd-famous either. I'm talking TV famous. And rich!"

The walls of the cavern slowly came into view as the cave narrowed. They could now see the enormous white limestone walls rising high above them.

"Finally, we are getting somewhere," Olivia said. "There must be a way out up here somewhere."

"Look, they climb too," Gnat said. On the cavern walls, urchins stuck to the rock. Doug leaned in close to one. He heard the urchin scraping into the limestone. Sand fell down into the water.

"They are making sand. They are scraping the rock and making sand," Doug said. "Could it be?" He looked up the wall. Sand was falling down. Lots of it. Each little urchin made the slightest bit, but together, by the thousands, a rain of sand fell. It drifted to the base of the wall and formed large mounds. Urchins on the cave floor plowed through the sand drifts, spreading it, pushing it out into the darkness.

"Everything scientists have written, everything in the books. . . . Don't you understand? They are making sand!" Doug stammered.

"Yeah, how cute," Olivia said.

"Extreme. Very extreme," Gnat agreed.

"You know what? You guys will see. You will see. These urchins probably made that big sand hill that we fell on. They probably made all of the sand in Florida!"

The walls narrowed, closer and closer as they walked. The cool water covered the sand, and soon the water was up to their ankles. The ceiling was still so far above them that they couldn't see it. It was like walking down a long, dark hallway.

"Maybe we should turn around, guys. I don't know about this," Doug said.

"Let's just see what is up here. There wasn't a way out back there," Olivia answered.

Suddenly, a thudding splash crashed behind them. Hundreds of urchins screamed and scattered into the water. They dropped off the walls by the thousands, splashing into the lake. There, in the middle of all them, an enormous eight-legged animal was plunging its head into the mass of urchins and scooping up mouthfuls. The urchins were squirting pink ink everywhere. The creature shook his head violently from side to side, sending the bitter ink splattering into the air. The urchins rushed into the deeper water. But they were no match for the giant predator.

"Nooooooo! Leave them alone!" Olivia screamed. She threw a handful of sand at it.

The animal raised its head up. It was larger than a horse, but the most amazing thing about it was its body was almost completely clear. They could see the heart and lungs inside, beating furiously. There were other specks and organs in there too. It stood on eight short, stumpy legs, thick as tree trunks. Its body looked like it was made of clear jelly, filled with water or corn syrup, stretching and changing shape like a snail. But its head is what sent a screeching jolt through Olivia. Rising up on its thick neck, the head had an enormous, toothless mouth. It towered over her. She could see the urchins rolling about in its wet, sticky maw. And she saw them swallowed with a gulp. Its eyes were pinpricks of solid black, the only dark part of its body. She couldn't tell where it was looking or where it would plunge down for another urchin mouthful.

"Leave them . . . alone!" Olivia screamed again. She flung another handful of wet sand. The creature turned toward her. The blasting noise that came out of its mouth burned in her ears. It started slowly sloshing toward her on its thick legs.

"Run, Gnat. Run!" Olivia screamed. She turned to run after the boys — then she suddenly remembered something. "Squirt! Squirt! Where are you?"

"SQUEAK!"

He hopped up in the ankle-deep water. Hearing the commotion, the clear beast lunged. Olivia scooped Squirt up just in time and fell backward as its huge head pounded into the ground near her feet. She stared into its tiny, cold eyes. There was no glimmer of mercy inside them. Olivia scrambled up to her feet and ran, shoving Squirt into her pocket. Huge waves rushed forward with every step of the creature. The monster was not a fast runner, but it moved easily in the shallow water.

As they sloshed along, the water slowly rose higher and higher, the cave walls pressed in closer and closer. Gnat was up to his waist. He was almost swimming.

And then, it ended.

The tombolo did not go any further. Worse than that, it was a dead-end.

"Now what do we do?" Doug yelled, overwhlemed by the sheer wall in front of him.

"Look. Over there. A hole." Olivia splashed over. There was a perfectly round hole bored directly into the limestone. Water was rushing down into the darkness. There were strange carvings all around the opening. At the top, a carving looked like a sun and a moon with another, smaller circle connecting them.

The gelatinous creature ran faster in the water than it did in the shallows. It finally caught up to them. There was nowhere to go. The creature filled the entire cavern. Olivia could feel Squirt shaking in her pocket.

"Go! Into the hole!" Olivia yelled. "Quick!"

"Are you kidding? We don't know where it goes," Doug said.

"Do you have a better idea?"

"Maybe we can fight it. We shouldn't go deeper."

"We don't have anything to fight with. Come on! Hurry!"

"No. I won't go."

The creature was almost on them.

"Aaaaaaaayahhhhhhh!" Olivia turned to see the top of Gnat's head disappearing into the hole.

"Gnat!" Olivia jumped after him. As she slid she managed to yell, "Doug! Come on!" But he didn't follow her, and for the second time that day, she felt herself disappearing into the dark unknown.

8

A Trillion Fireflies

Water rushed all around as she slid down the tube.

"Gnat! Gnat!" she yelled. "Are you there?"

"Weeeeeeeeeeeeeeee!" She heard him somewhere below having entirely too much fun. The slide turned and twisted and spun her around. Soon it leveled off and it was completely dark. Darker than anything Olivia had ever seen. Darker than the basement and even darker than when she shut her eyes under the covers.

"Gnat," she whispered. "Gnat, where are you?"

"Over here," he responded, snapping on the flashlight. Its dim light flickered.

"I can't believe it still works. Here, give it to me." Olivia took the light and swung it around. The water lit up as the faint beam penetrated the clear pool. To Olivia's amazement, when she moved the flashlight, the water stayed lit, glowing, as if a trillion fireflies were swimming around them. The glowing water spread out, and suddenly the entire pool of water was ablaze in bluish-green light.

They hardly had time to be surprised, because the newly lit cavern looked more like the remains of an ancient city than a cave. Instead of spreading out flat like most cities, this one was built almost straight up. It went so far up that Olivia was surprised she couldn't see the sky up at the top. There were grand facades carved into the cavern walls. There were porticos and arches, enormous columns and buttresses. Staircases spiraled upward. Terraces curved around buildings. A broad staircase descended straight down into the pool that they were sitting in.

"Come on, Gnat. Let's get out of the water."

"I concur," he said.

The city didn't look like the Roman or Greek ruins that Olivia had seen in school books. It appeared to be built the same way giant seashells are built. Most of it was a stark, bleached white material. It had the whorls and peaks of a periwinkle, the twists of a whelk. But they could see some faded, old decorative features, like the pink and purple enameling of a conch. The doorways were rounded. None of the windows were rectangular or even a shape that Olivia could describe. Mother-of-pearl layered over the railings. The doorways themselves were made of a thin, semi-transparent membrane, like a shell's operculum. She tried to push one of the doors open but it wouldn't budge. Water dripped, puddled, and streamed through the city in elaborate aqueducts, riverines, waterfalls, fountains, and pipes.

"Hello?" Olivia yelled. "Hello! Is anyone here?" Her voice echoed.

The pool of water behind them started to grow dim. She turned the flashlight into the water and it lit up once again.

"I have an idea," Gnat said, reaching for the flashlight. He walked over to one of the aqueducts, put the flashlight directly over it, and snapped it on. They watched as the bluish-green light ran up the duct, spreading into all of the waterways and pipes of the city. Bulbous streetlights lit up. Verandas high above the pool were lit from within. Waterfalls became cascades of light. Even the water that dripped from pipes high above fell like shooting stars down through the dark cave.

"Let's find someplace to dry off." Olivia started walking higher into the city. Squirt followed them, climbing up every stair and ramp. "I'm hungry."

"Me too. I hope Doug is OK. I like him," Gnat said.

"Me too. Wait a second." Olivia started rummaging through the backpack. "Here it is." She pulled out the Aquaman walkie-talkie. "You try it."

Gnat took the walkie-talkie in his small hands and looked at Olivia. He turned on the power and pushed down the talk-button. "Hello? Come in. Hello? Dougeeeee."

Nothing but static.

"Doug . . . eeeeee. It's Gnat."

Silence.

"Doug," Gnat snapped. "Pick . . . up . . . this is Aquaman."

"He probably didn't turn his on. I'm sure he got away from that horrible thing." But inside, Olivia was worried. Very worried. "Just leave it on in case he calls us." She pushed on every operculum as they walked by. Finally, one opened. Despite its light weight, the weird door seemed very strong.

"Is anyone home?" It was obvious that no one had lived there for a long time. Mushrooms seemed to be growing everywhere. Pale, clear mosses filled the corners. Delicate feathery ferns furled and unfurled like they were breathing. The floors undulated and inclined in a deliberate manner, as if to funnel water a certain way. She could see no boards or nails. There were no decorations or furniture that you would expect in a home. There were no pictures, couches, or clocks. There were no carpets, televisions, or lamps. Instead, there were shelves upon shelves of strangely shaped glass bottles, most of them empty, the contents dried to dust from the ravages of time. Some bottles were filled with colorful liquids: red, orange, and green. One was filled with round, white stones. One with cottony fluff. One held the preserved exoskeleton of a weird crablike creature. One twinkled with pink sparkles. Gnat reached up and pulled out the cork. The pink sparkles flew out of the opening like suddenly freed insects. They swirled around Gnat's head for a few seconds, spun up toward the ceiling like a slow, backwards tornado, then out through the door. Gnat jumped up and grabbed the last sparkle. It wriggled and tickled inside his fist before finding a way out between his fingers and following the others up into the darkness.

Olivia looked closely into one particularly large glass bottle. Inside, she saw herself. Or approximately herself. Smaller for sure, but there was something different about her too. The tiny girl looked back at her. She had her eyes. Her hair was longer, maybe. Or her nose was a little too wide. The bottle girl pressed her tiny hands up against the thick glass. Then she curled up on a bed, her same ancient enormous bed, and fell asleep in the Milligans' house. Olivia shook her head hard.

"Gnat, take a look at this," she said.

Gnat looked. The bottle was empty.

"But there . . . never mind." Olivia put the bottle back on the shelf.

Squirt was in the corner, enthusiastically munching mushrooms.

"Squirt sure is a pig," Gnat said. "At least *he* gets to eat."

"I haven't seen any more cave urchins since we slid down the tunnel. Poor little Squirt. He is lost from home too. I wonder who used to live here."

"I think it's aliens," Gnat stated.

Almost every road in the town was really a staircase, most of them crooked or spiraling up the cave wall. They followed what must have been the main boulevard because the bulbous street lights lined both sides. It was an exhausting climb. Olivia couldn't imagine a steeper city. As they came around a particularly precarious ramp, they saw a large clear wall holding back a deep water source, a cistern of sorts. Light shimmered through the water. There must have been millions of gallons of water held back by the transparent wall.

"Do you even have a watch?"

"Negative."

"Well, I'm tired. Let's rest here," Olivia suggested. "It's dry and doesn't look like anyone lives here."

They sat down against the clear wall. The wall wasn't hard like glass. It flexed as her back pushed into it like a giant vertical waterbed. Gnat leaned on Olivia's shoulder. Squirt nestled under her neck.

"I love you, Livia," Gnat murmured.

"Love ya, Gnatty."

"Goodnight Doug," Gnat spoke into the walkie-talkie. Olivia grabbed his hand. And with that, they both fell asleep.

9

The Tardigrade

Doug watched Olivia jump into the watery hole and he hoped it wasn't the last time he would see her. Parts of him wanted to jump after her and Gnat — the part that was afraid and the part that wanted to protect his friends, if he could. But something bigger was telling him to stay. Stay and fight with everything he had. The beast swung its head and knocked Doug into the cave wall and any thought of escaping disappeared. He was in a fight for his life. Doug tried to punch back, but the beast was too fast and too strong. He hit it once, but it didn't seem to have any effect. Its flesh was tougher than it looked. Doug backed up, farther and farther until he was in the final corner at the end of the cave. The water was now up to his neck. The creature loomed over him. Doug stared deep into its chest, past the heart. He thought he could see a stomach filled with urchins in there. The creature stunk. It made him sick to his stomach.

Doug grew dizzy and he stumbled. Now there was no escape. There was nothing left to try. He panicked. He started yelling as loudly as he could.

"No! NO! NO!"

Suddenly, his mouth changed the words.

"Goran!" he screamed. It made no sense. What kind of word was that? His brain must be shutting down and this was going to be his last moment on Earth. He tried to shout "No!" once more, but it came out all wrong this time too.

"Goran!"

And quite unexpectedly, the creature stopped advancing. It sat down with an enormous splash.

There are some things in life, words, dreams, fears, that come from places inside of us that we do not understand. Some say they come from the past, some say we all share these common experiences. Some say they are words that we must have heard at some point in our infancy. Some even say that these words and dreams are stored in our DNA as relics of an unknown history. Needless to say, however, only a very few people ever experience the emergence of these experiences from the past. It only happens to sensitive people. People who are open to the impossible. Or impossibly scared.

Doug could command the creature! He didn't know how, and he didn't even know what he was trying to say. It just happened.

"Syphlan ni phorone"

The creature lowered its head and extended its neck. Doug could tell it wanted him to jump on its back. Slowly, Doug advanced toward the creature. The smell grew stronger as he approached. Gently, he put his hands against the creature's neck. Its flesh was firm and cold. Grabbing hold of a flap of clear flesh, Doug lunged his legs upward and over the back. He couldn't believe he was now riding atop the very creature that he hated so much, the merciless predator of the cave urchins. It rose up, taking Doug high above the waterline.

"Syphlan ni carban chtuk."

With that, the creature turned and started making its way back along the tombolo. It had a gentle gait, smooth and comfortable. Doug thought of Olivia and Gnat down that hole. Then he remembered the Aquaman walkie-talkie. It had been jammed into his pocket for so long that he had forgotten all about it. He pulled it out and pushed the button.

"Hello? Hello? Gnat? Olivia? Can you hear me?"

Nothing but static. If they were in trouble down there, if they were hurt or impossibly lost, then he was their only hope. If he went down after them, he could be lost too. Doug knew that he had to get to the surface himself, to go and get help.

The monster moved smoothly, almost effortlessly through the water. Doug looked down and saw the remains of many cave urchins where the monster had fed earlier. The pink ink slowly dispersed into the water. Instead of staying on the tombolo, the monster turned and entered the vast lake.

"Wait! I know what you are. You are a tardigrade!" Doug yelled with excitement. "You are kind of big though." Doug's laughter rang throughout the cave. The creature ignored him.

Tardigrades were one of the last experiments that his Dad ever showed him. Dad had said that schools refused to teach about tardigrades, and that he was "obligated by the Truth" to show Doug. Dad had pulled out a clump of lichen from a tree stump and shook it in some water until it turned into a murky soup. Under a microscope, the lichen soup came alive with thousands of marvelous creatures. The finest creature of them all, however, was the tardigrade. Most of the microscopic life shimmied and slimed its way like worms or motorboats. But tardigrades walk on legs, like a bear, even if they have eight instead of four. They have faces. They are cute. Doug didn't realize at the time how mean they could be.

Those tardigrades were the size of pinpricks. This one towered over Doug.

The giant tardigrade swam along the cave wall, and soon Doug could see countless passageways in the rock. All along, Olivia, Gnat, and he had stayed on the tombolo and never saw the cave wall. They had thought there was only one direction to go.

Doug peeked into each tunnel as they passed by. Who had made these? Was it the urchins as they chewed the rock into sand? Some of the tunnels were huge. Too huge for urchins. Many of the entrances had markings that Doug couldn't understand. The tardigrade decided to turn into one of the marked tunnels. How it decided on this particular tunnel, Doug didn't know. Maybe he had commanded it with those odd words. He certainly didn't know where they were going. Hopefully, it wasn't taking him back to be devoured by a nest of baby tardigrades.

Now they were swimming in the dark. A single antler emerged and grew out of the top of the tardigrade's head. The knob on the top of the antler glowed a yellowish light. The tunnel walls were smooth, very smooth. The antler-light reflected on the walls like they were made of glass. This wasn't anything like the caverns that he saw when he visited his grandma up in Marianna. The Florida Caverns were made of limestone and had stalagmites and stalactites.

The thought of Marianna made him sad. His mom must be worried sick. "I'll bet she called the cops," he thought. "She's always calling cops." Whenever the Mutches at school got too rough, Mrs. Corcoran would call the sheriff and demand that they do something about it. Doug hated that because it only made the un-twins meaner the next day. She even tried to get the Mutches to pay the dental bill when they knocked out his tooth. He remembered the smirk on Larry's face when Mr. Mutch slammed the door in her face. Boy, he would love to see the looks on their faces when he pulled up to school riding a ferocious tardigrade.

Soon the water ran out. The tardigrade didn't start walking though. It slid like a seal or an otter along the smooth floor. It slid to the left when they came to a fork. It slid down a tunnel in the floor then slid up a tunnel in the ceiling. Sometimes the tunnel was so narrow, that the tardigrade squished down until Doug was almost standing on the ground again. Sometimes Doug had to duck. Tunnels were going by in a blur. Down one of the tunnels, Doug swore he saw another tardigrade going the other direction, its glowing antler disappearing around a corner. He reached out to the wall. Its smoothness slipped along his fingers like a block of ice. A bit of slime stuck to his fingers. They passed through an enormous room filled with white grasses and clear animals grazing. Some of them had arms like squid. Some had enormous, porcelain eyes. They slid by so fast Doug wasn't even sure what he saw.

And then the tardigrade stopped.

"Gronk," it announced with a brassy voice. Doug didn't move. Was it calling someone else or telling him something?

"Gronk!" it repeated. Then its body started tilting, knocking Doug from its back at the entrance to a tunnel of stairs. The glowing antler detached from the tardigrade's head and dropped to his feet.

Doug stood up and brushed himself off and picked up the antler. He patted the side of the tardigrade and said "Gronk."

"That was stupid," he thought. "I probably just told him to get off me." Doug tried hard to think of some special words for thank you, some words that it could understand. But his mind was blank. He didn't know what to say. The tardigrade started turning toward him menacingly. On its head, another glowing antler started to emerge.

"Oh, here we go again," Doug thought as he ran up the tunnel hoping it led to the surface. "Thanks for the ride!"

10

Chapel of Light

When they woke up, the city lights were almost out. Gnat walked over to the nearest aqueduct to ignite the city again. The flashlight wouldn't turn on. He shook it as hard as he could until a pale yellow glimmer glowed from the bulb. The faint light lit the water before the flashlight snapped and popped and broke down for good. The city lights were barely at half power.

"Come on, we have a lot of climbing to do," Olivia said. "We have to get out of here before we run out of light or we will never escape."

Gnat was too tired to argue. The cave stopped being incredible a long time ago. Olivia knew he just wanted to sit at the kitchen table and eat the biggest bowl of Crunchberry imaginable or at least a bag of mega-sour candy. For what seemed like hours, they climbed up the twisting streets and stairways. They passed what looked like libraries and houses, marketplaces and laboratories. They climbed up and over what was surely City Hall. They walked by buildings that couldn't be described in words that mean something to humans. Olivia just focused on going up and coaxing Gnat ahead of her. They knew that "up" was where home was. Up was where they would find food and a warm shower.

Eventually, they came to the top. The very edge of the city. There were no more ramps or stairs to climb. If they took one more step they would go tumbling far down to the pool below. There wasn't even a guardrail. Olivia looked across the chasm. A beautiful building was on the other side. The most beautiful building they had seen yet. It looked like a church with elaborate carvings and spires. The operculum was a rich golden color. But there was no bridge.

Next to the cliff was a large shell mounted on an ivory post. It was the largest shell they had ever seen. Each of its edges shone with silver.

"We need to figure out a way to get over there. Any ideas, Squirt?" Olivia asked.

"SQUEAK!" Squirt jumped up and spun around.

"Me neither. How 'bout you, Gnat?"

"Level requires secret key," Gnat said.

"This isn't a video game. . . ." Olivia snapped. "Wait a second. You're brilliant, Gnat! There must be a key around here somewhere." She looked all around.

Gnat wandered back to the last building they had passed to search for a key inside. Olivia examined the ivory post and shell. She noticed three small indentations on one side of the post. The shape of the indentations looked familiar.

"I got it!" Olivia screamed taking the necklace off her neck. Each of the beads, the three beads that the coral snakes gave her, fit perfectly into the indentations. Black, yellow, red. She made sure the yellow bead was in the middle. Holding them against the post with her right hand, a warm glow flowed into her skin. She was expecting a bridge suddenly to appear from above or to slide out from underneath them. Instead, the silver cap that covered the small end of the shell slowly slid away.

"Hmmmm." Olivia put her mouth to the small end of the shell and blew. A deep moaning note echoed out into the cavern.

"Hey! Cool! Let me try," Gnat ordered, pushing her out of the way. The note blew out again, rolling down the dark corridors and passageways of the city like a foghorn on some foggy shore. Again and again, they took turns.

And then, something answered.

Sonorous and mellow, a noise not unlike a whale-song rose up from the darkness.

"Uh oh," Gnat whispered.

A large, fleshy animal slowly emerged in the water far below. It resembled a garden slug, except it was mottled with spots and had long, undulating wings made of skin that ran along the entire length of its body. Its head was covered with bumps and protuberances. An Anaspidean.

Olivia blew the shell horn again. Gnat hid behind her.

This time, the large creature sang out, and his entire body shivered so hard that water splashed up from the vibrations. His fleshy wings undulated like the waves of the sea rippling along his body. Faster and faster until they were just a blur. He took one enormous breath.

Slowly, the Anaspidean rose up from the water and into the air like a dirigible. Great buckets of water flowed off his vast back. Past the stairways, past the library, past City Hall, he rose like a living hot air balloon. The bridge horn sounded again and he let out a bellow filled with so much exuberance that the entire cave rung. Olivia and Gnat could hear bottles crashing off their shelves from all of the vibrating noise. They covered their ears with their hands. Slowly, the Anaspidean rose, singing. His large eyes rolled in his head.

Finally, he reached Olivia and Gnat. He extended the soft rim of his body so it spanned the entire chasm.

"A bridge!" Gnat yelled out stepping onto the edge of the great animal. With each spongy step, a splash of color circled out across his flesh. It felt like jelly under their feet. The Anaspidean cooed and purred as the children scrambled across his back. Gnat looked down to the glowing pool far below. Squirt scooted quickly across the creature's back, afraid of falling.

Reaching the doorstep of the chapel, Olivia turned, knelt down, and gently rubbed the Anaspidean's soft skin. "Thank you," she said loudly so he could hear. His large eye turned toward her. Olivia could see her reflection in his cornea. He joyously bellowed one last time, so loudly that Olivia and Gnat covered their ears and still went momentarily deaf. With that, he released his grip and slowly began his descent. In the darkness of the pool, he swam once again into the vast Florida aquifer. Looking down into the chasm, Olivia could see that the lights were going out. The darkness was rising up toward them. She had to act fast or they would be trapped here forever.

The operculum in front of them was even more beautiful now that they were close. Pearls hung in long strings around the ornate opening. Calcite crystals grew in beautiful clusters. Obviously it was the most important building in the whole town. There were strange words and symbols carved into the doorway. Gnat pushed on the operculum. It wouldn't budge. He pushed harder. Nothing happened. How were they going to get in? Now they were really in a bad spot if they couldn't get the door to open. The bridge horn was on the other side of the chasm. They only had a few feet of space to stand on. Olivia pushed against the operculum. It suddenly opened easily.

"You need to go to door-opening school, Gnat," Olivia laughed.

Inside was a large white room filled with quiet, terraced pools and twinkling lights. There was a lot of dust as if the room hadn't been used in years or decades. Maybe longer. The walls were covered from ceiling to floor with strange symbols and markings.

An enormous pearly wheel stuck up out of the floor. Gnat couldn't resist. Putting both hands on it, he pushed with all of his might and turned it. A rusty groan vibrated through the whole building. After a few rotations, the wheel moved more and more easily. A thick, clear lens slowly lowered from the high ceiling. The lens was as big as a boat. Gnat spun the wheel faster and faster. Finally, as the wheel stopped turning, the lens tilted. A thin shaft of sunlight suddenly shot down from the ceiling. As the lens tilted, it intersected through the pale beam of light that shone down from the surface. A thin, powerful beam shot out from the other side of the lens like a laser, striking the terraced pools of water. The water filled with blaring light and quickly spread out of the chapel into the city below. Olivia and Gnat ran to the operculum and looked down. They watched as the light flowed down the aqueducts and waterfalls, circling down into the darkness. The city lit brighter than ever. Somehow, in this chapel, the inhabitants were able to capture the weak sunlight from high above and ignite the city.

"So that is how they did it," she whispered.

"Did what?" Gnat asked.

"Collected the light. They didn't have flashlights. I'm sure of it. Each morning in church, they must have turned this wheel. I'll bet we are close to the surface."

"That could be my job," Gnat announced proudly.

"Yeah . . ." Olivia was looking the other way. "You are the official wheel-turner. . . ." Her voice trailed off.

Near the back of the room, a pedestal stood on a dais. Perched on top of the pedestal was a glowing blue sphere the size of a cantaloupe. It was the same blue color of the light rays streaming down on the tombolo yesterday. Like sunlight in a spring.

"Livia . . . Livia." Gnat tugged at her arm, but she didn't hear him. She stared at the blue sphere, slowly walking toward it. She stepped up onto the dais and set her backpack down on the ground

"Olivia!"

She pushed his arm back and reached out. The sphere was calling to her. As her fingers barely brushed its surface, it started to hum and twinkle like bells. It felt warm. She held her hands to the heat. Olivia wanted to wrap around it like a cat. She wanted to fly headlong into it like a moth. She pressed her palm onto it. She could feel the humming in her bones. It was smooth as vanilla ice cream on the tongue. Her eyes widened. She looked deep into its color, and to her it suddenly wasn't blue at all. She could see so many other colors. And there was more. So much more.

"O . . . livia!" Gnat finally pulled hard enough to knock her off the dais. "Let's go!" To the left was a stairway with a sun symbol carved over it. Gnat pulled her toward the entrance as she adjusted her backpack. Squirt stopped at the stairs. He wouldn't go any farther.

"SQUEAK!" He hopped.

"Come on, Squirt."

"SQUEAK!" He turned around and shuffled back toward the operculum.

"He wants to stay."

Olivia reached down and picked Squirt up. "Come with us, I'll keep you safe." But Squirt jumped and squirmed so hard that she was forced to put him down. "Goodbye, Squirt. Be careful, I guess you don't belong on the surface." Olivia kissed the star on his back and he flushed pink light.

"Bye, Squirt. Rock on," Gnat said.

They stepped through the entrance with the sun above it and a door slammed behind them. Olivia knew the door was sealed shut. There would be no going back.

Before them was a stairway that was different from the ones back in the city. It was made from rough stone. It was narrow and dirty. It seemed like a secret, not a passageway that anyone would use on a regular basis. The lighting was dim, almost too dim.

Olivia and Gnat struggled with every step. The straps of the backpack were digging into her shoulders. Her legs were burning. The stairway took sharp turns, but it never stopped going upward. They saw a light up above.

"Hurry, Gnat! I see a light." Their pace quickened as they raced upward and turned the corner.

"Hi, guys." It was Doug!

"Dougee!" Gnat ran to him and hugged his leg.

"What happened? Where did you go?"

"We tried calling you . . . Aquaman . . . it didn't work."

"I was riding the tardigrade."

"Tardi . . . who?" Olivia asked.

"The creature. I rode it."

"Well, there was a city and the water was glowing and Squirt didn't come with us but he is fine." Gnat was talking a mile-a-minute.

"I rode it, like a horse." Doug didn't think they heard him. "I almost died."

"And the street lights were made of water and there was a giant flying bridge and the bridge was an animal bigger than a whale and . . . what is that?" Olivia asked, pointing to the glowing antler.

"It grew out of the tardigrade and he gave it to me."

Gnat and Olivia stared at him.

"Did you hit your head?" Olivia didn't know whether to laugh or be concerned.

"It's true, and I rode him."

"OK, we have to get you to a doctor. Let's get out of here."

Long, thin tree roots were hanging down from the ceiling like spaghetti and they had to push their way through the tangled mess. Once in a while, a root would be so big that they had to press up against the wall to slide by. They came to a landing. A small tunnel slanted upwards. Olivia went first, then Gnat and Doug. The tunnel was so narrow, they could barely move. Olivia clawed and scratched her way upwards, pushing roots out of the way with her hands. She crawled her way upward inch by inch. Dirt clogged her fingernails. Her face was covered with grime and sweat. Her hands reached out ahead and found the top of the tunnel. She looked up. Stars! The moon! They had made it! Energized, she pulled herself out onto the sandy ground. She reached back down and lifted Gnat out, and finally Doug.

They looked back. They had just crawled out of a tortoise burrow. One of Doug's flags stuck up out of the sand only a few feet away.

"There are no such things as stairs in tortoise burrows," Doug said with an eyebrow raised.

"Well, there aren't supposed to be giant clear monsters and cave urchins either," Olivia reminded him.

"I rode it, you know," he said sheepishly.

"I'm starving," she said.

"I have no idea where we are," Doug said, holding the antler over his head.

Then the tardigrade antler suddenly dimmed and shriveled to a dry powder in his hands.

"Huh?" he exclaimed. "I wanted to keep that."

"Well, we better start walking if we ever want to get home."

But they barely took one step when they heard something nearby breathing. Something big.

"Li . . . Livia?" Gnat stammered. "It's that bear."

The enormous bear, the one that started the whole thing back at the spring, sat on his haunches watching them. A bag of white bread hung in the bear's mouth. The kids froze. They were too tired to run. How could he possibly have known where they were going to come out of the cave? They were miles from where they had disappeared into the burrow. He was also bigger than they remembered. His black fur disappeared into the shadows of the night, but they could hear him breathing and see his cinnamon tuft of hair glistening in the starlight.

The bear dropped the bag of bread to the ground and swatted it toward them. Olivia slowly reached down and picked up the bag. The kids tore into the loaf, devouring every crumb. The bear watched them gulp down the slices of bread.

"Thank you, Mr. Bear," Gnat said with a crust hanging from his lips.

"Thunder," Olivia said smacking her lips. "His name is Thunder."

Plain, white bread never tasted so good. She didn't even miss peanut butter.

It became clear that Thunder was not interested in hurting them. In fact, he seemed friendly. Olivia threw him a handful of slices.

"How . . . how did he find us," Doug wondered aloud.

"Thunder must like us because of the beads the snakes gave me," Olivia whispered. "Think about it. Mr. Gruffle. You said tortoises don't do that. The alligator. It must be the beads."

"What are you talking about?" Doug answered.

"The coral snakes under the house. They gave me these. And not only that, the beads opened the bridge horn down there that called the bridge whale up out of the water."

"All right. For the very last time I'm going to tell you," he said raising his fingers in the air, "there are nooooo such things as . . ."

"Is it *really* so hard to believe?" Olivia cut him off. "I mean after all we've been through? You sound just like my uncle."

"Well, snakes don't have pockets. How to do they carry beads around with them?" Doug said definitively.

"Why don't you crawl under the house and ask them? Listen, no one is going to believe us about where we were all this time. Swear never to tell. We need to figure this out."

"No way! We discovered something. We are going to be famous. We discovered new animals. I'm sure of it. It is everything I've been looking for. No, it's *way* more than I was looking for."

Olivia turned to Doug, her eyes blazing. "Doug. Listen. I'm not saying we can't *ever* tell. I'm not saying we won't be famous. I'm saying that there is something bigger happening. I can feel it. Think about it, a bear is helping us! A *bear* . . . brought us. . . . *bread*." She pointed at the beast and raised the empty bag up into the air. "Isn't it worth waiting so we can figure this out? Please promise me."

They stood in silence for a few minutes. Doug looked up. "All right," he said. "But my Mom is going to want to know what happened to my clipboard and the flags. Not to mention where I've been all this time."

"Tell her we got lost."

"Hmmmm. I'm not so sure she'll buy that. I've lived here my whole life."

"Tell her it was my fault." Her fingers were digging into his arm so hard it bruised.

"OK! I won't say anything. Sheesh!"

"Thank you, Nature Boy." Olivia smiled. It made Doug feel good inside to see Olivia smiling.

Thunder stood up. His head towered over them. He swung around and started walking the opposite direction. After a couple of steps, he looked back at the kids, huffed loudly, and shook his head.

"I think he wants us to follow him," Olivia said.

"Bears don't do that," Doug said.

Olivia just stared at him.

"Okay," she said. "Gnat and I are going with Thunder. You can sit out here with the Mutch twins and the Bobwhite Witch and write your essay on how bears are supposed to act. We'll come for you in the morning."

Olivia put her right hand on Thunder's back. She dug her fingers deep into his wiry thick fur. She could feel his tough leg muscles working under his skin. With her other hand, she grabbed Gnat. And off they went into the dark scrub. Doug ran to catch up and grabbed Gnat's free hand.

Olivia would later learn that there are countless miles of hidden highways that bears use to travel long distances, giving them access to important areas without being seen. Bear highways lead to springs, the palmetto berry feeding grounds, nearby bee hives, gopher apple patches, and the local dump. Some of the highways lead all the way down to the Everglades and all the way up to Okefenokee. The highways are impossible to find if you do not know the secret signs. They disappear into the thickest of palmetto tangles. They run out of sight of any houses or interstate. The bears only rarely have to come out into a clearing or cross roads. In fact, almost no humans have even heard of these highways, much less traveled on one.

Thunder pushed through the thorny thicket. Olivia found that if she kept her hand on his back and just kept walking, no matter how tangled and impassable it looked ahead, that she would somehow get through it all without a scratch. If she paid too much attention or tried to avoid the oncoming brush, she would get smacked in the face with a branch or a thorn would catch her leg. Once, she lifted her hand from Thunder so she could scratch her nose, and suddenly she was lost. Thunder had disappeared in the palmettos ahead of her and she didn't know where to walk. The spiny fronds snagged her shirt and stabbed into her skin. They were stuck in the middle of the thicket with no way out. In a few minutes, Thunder came back and found them. He looked at her as if to say, "Don't let go again." Olivia felt a simple, pure affinity for the old bear. For some reason, she trusted him.

Things worked best if she simply closed her eyes, dug her fingers in, and let him pull her along the highway. She could hear Doug squawking and yelping even though she had yelled back to him and Gnat to not look where they are going. "He just won't learn," she thought to herself, laughing.

"Are we there yet?" Gnat yelled.

"I don't know," Olivia yelled back. Thunder seemed to pick up the pace whenever he heard them talking. One thing bears do not seem to tolerate is laziness, and the fact that the she had enough energy to talk meant that she had enough energy to walk faster. For hours they plunged through the scrub. She wanted to stop and rest more than anything, but Thunder compelled her forward. Sometimes, they would see the porch lights from a house. Once, a large dog lunged against his chain, yelping and snarling as they passed. Thunder just ignored all of it. They walked along a remote road, just inside the brushy woods. A few cars whizzed by. Once Thunder decided it was safe, he took a sharp turn to the left and they rushed across the pavement. Olivia could see some truck headlights in the distance. Doug let go of Gnat's hand and stopped in the middle of the road.

"Hey! Over here!" he yelled, jumping up and down.

"Doug! No!" Olivia yelled back. She pulled on Thunder's fur to tell him to stop. He looked back and shook his head. He turned quickly, ran back to Doug, and pushed him across the road with his nose. He pushed so hard it was as more like he picked Doug up and flung him into the safety of the woods. Standing over him, Thunder huffed so loudly that Doug could feel the bear's breath rush through his hair. He got the message. He stood up sheepishly, wiping the dirt from his arms. Doug was beginning to wonder if they were being kidnapped by a bear. The truck sped by and disappeared into the night.

They started walking again, plunging headlong through the forest. It seemed like they had been walking for days. Just when Olivia thought that her legs would fall off, Thunder stopped. Olivia looked ahead. There, just over the fence, was the Milligans' house. She had never been so happy to see a familiar sight.

"Hey!" she yelled. "We are home!"

Suddenly, a dozen flashlights swung through the darkness and settled on them. After spending so long in the dark woods, the bright lights burned their eyes. What happened next was complete chaos. Olivia could see flashing blue and red lights from several police cars. Men started yelling, "Over here! They are over here! We found them!"

Thunder took several menacing steps forward, putting himself between the kids and the strange men. He huffed as loudly as he could and snapped his jaws. For the first time, Olivia saw his teeth. The thick fur on his back bristled and he pushed his ears back onto his head. He was ready to fight. The call went out. "Bear! Bear!" Men ran to their trucks and grabbed their rifles. A helicopter suddenly switched on its spotlight. The trees blew and twisted in all directions. Flying sand stung Olivia's eyes. Several crates of hunting dogs were released. They were yelping and kicking up dirt as they raced toward them. Thunder huffed again, slapping his paw toward the dogs.

Olivia leaned in close to his ear and yelled, "Run Thunder. Run! We will be all right!" She held his face and kissed him on the muzzle. She looked deep into his big eyes. "Go!" He turned around and crashed into the dark forest with the pack of dogs at his heels. The men with guns followed, some riding ATVs. Olivia jumped at the legs of one of the men.

"No! Leave him alone! Leave him alone!" She was crying and holding onto the hunter's foot. "Doug, stop them!"

Cheeto stormed out of the house and was pulling as hard as he could on the pant leg of another man. But there were too many. The hunters pushed right through, and in a few moments all they could hear were the dogs baying in the distance. She grabbed Gnat and held him close, whispering, "Please get away, Thunder. Please."

Aunt, Uncle, Doug's mother, and half of Lyonia surrounded them, all talking at once. Olivia could see where Doug got his nerdiness from. His mother had an old hairstyle and horn-rimmed glasses. Uncle scooped Olivia and Gnat up in his arms and marched triumphantly toward the house. Olivia twisted around to say goodbye to Doug, but his mother had grabbed his collar, and was steering him to their car. Olivia pulled back the curtains and looked out as they drove away. At least *his* mother was there for him. She saw several TV vans in the yard with satellite dishes extended high above the trees. The TV cameras were lit with bright lights. She could see news reporters with microphones standing with their backs to the house and talking to the cameras. Police cars came and went. There were pickup trucks parked everywhere. Some looked a hundred years old with handmade bumpers welded on their backsides and doors that appeared to have originated on different cars altogether. Some trucks had extra wheels and elaborate paint jobs. The police lights reflected off all the chrome.

"Just great, we won't even be able to watch ourselves on TV," Olivia humphed.

Aunt was sitting on the couch cradling Gnat in her arms. "Are you hurt? Are you hurt?" she kept repeating.

"No, we are fine," Olivia answered.

"All systems are go," Gnat said. "We were lost!" Olivia punched him.

"Are you hurt? Maybe you are hurt. Harold, we should take them to the hospital. Harold! *Get over here.* They might be hurt."

"Really, we are fine. We just want to take a shower."

"Well, we are going to fix one of those TVs and buy some batteries. Don't you ever . . . I mean it, don't you ever . . . do that again. We are so happy that you are all right. We are blessed. You aren't hurt are you?" Aunt was teetering between joy, exhaustion, worry, and anger. She was crying. Gnat started crying. Olivia thought about Squirt down in the caves with thousands of his brothers and sisters. She thought about Thunder and she prayed hard that he escaped. And Uncle just sat quietly in the corner chair with his feet up on the stool, watching them.

11

A Secret

The next morning, Olivia awoke to find one thousand small, faintly green moths arranged neatly on her bedroom window. She knew there were one thousand because she began to count and only made it to 45 before she realized that she hadn't even counted all of the moths in one tiny corner. She tapped the glass and they all fluttered off into the forest. The sun suddenly burst through her window. The dust danced in the rays, twinkling with old stories and legends that only the dust knows. All of the hunters, policemen, and TV announcers had left during the night. Olivia looked out the window and saw that the coral snakes had forged a new path over the tire tracks and boot prints that had been left in the sand. When Olivia walked out of her room, she saw Uncle in the living room tinkering with an old television set. Cheeto followed her every step. Whenever she paused, he stopped and stared at her.

"Well, I'll be. Cheeto likes you. He won't have anything to do with me," Uncle said.

"I guess he missed me. What are you doing?" she asked, rubbing her eyes.

Uncle looked up at her. His tiny eyes sparkled on his face. "I'm fixing this TV."

"Turn it on, turn it on!"

"Your aunt believes," he said pointing his screwdriver toward the kitchen, "that you two ran away because we do not have a TV."

"That isn't right. We didn't run away."

"She knows you have been through a lot. It must be hard to adjust to a new place. You know, it's hot down here. We don't have snow. We probably don't have enough cheese."

Olivia smiled. "We didn't run away. This crazy . . . um . . . house is even all right. I don't even know why we are here. Dad never told us and he hasn't even called."

"Well, I can't really say what is going on with your Dad. I don't know. I would tell you if I did," he said, still digging around in the middle of the television set. "But I do know that your aunt and I are both very happy that you are here. You and Nathan are welcome to stay here as long as it takes. I also know, . . ." he paused, "that we can't let you two go running around the woods like a couple of wild bobcats."

"We weren't running around wild. We were flagging tortoises. I mean burrows. Tortoise burrows. They're endangered, you know. We got lost. Thund. . . . the bear brought us home. He was nice to us. He even brought us bread to eat."

Uncle raised an eyebrow. "See, the way I figure it, there is more to the story than you are telling us. You know I can't help you if you don't tell me the truth."

"Well, it's true. We got lost." Olivia stared at her feet.

"Deputy McDaniel told me yesterday that they found children's tracks and blood on the rocks down by Bluejack Springs. They even put a diver down into the water because they thought y'all might have drowned. Do you know anything about that?"

Olivia's mind raced. Her throat hurt so much she couldn't speak.

"Your aunt and I decided that you and Gnat should go to summer school."

"What!? Summer school? But my grades are good," Olivia interrupted.

"Me?!" yelled Gnat. "I already passed first grade!"

"You are smart, Olivia. Smarter than I was at your age. And as for you, young man, the school has given us permission to enroll you too — for enrichment. I am obligated to make sure you are both safe. I can't imagine calling your mother and telling her that you were hurt. Besides, summer school is fun. It starts in two weeks and it will give you some-thing to do," he said, lifting the television upright. "In the meantime, I'd appreciate it if you two stuck around the house."

"What's enrichment?" Gnat had his arms crossed and looked ready to explode.

"It means 'no more video games,'" Olivia responded. Gnat quickly turned red.

"Nonsense," Uncle jumped in. "It means fun. It means you can make new friends and . . . and have fun." Uncle had a look of hopeful pleading in his eyes.

Gnat seemed to consider their words carefully before yawning and heading toward his room.

"That was close." Uncle breathed a sigh of relief.

"I can't believe he bought it. Summer school is no one's idea of fun."

"Come on, Olivia, let's see if this old thing works.

The way Uncle talked to her, like she was an adult, made her punish-ment seem not so bad. The truth is, she didn't really want to go out there in the woods again anyway. Not after what they just went through. At least for now. Except maybe to see Thunder or Squirt.

As soon as Uncle plugged in the television, a huge spark and puff of smoke erupted into the room. Olivia could smell burnt dust. After adjusting some dials and the antenna, a wavy picture came into focus.

"We have a TV! Gnat!" she squealed down the hallway. "We have a TV!" Gnat opened his door yawning, walked straight out and sat in front of the TV, staring at the screen. They played with the channel knob.

"Wow, two whole channels."

Gnat didn't seem to care. One channel was enough for him. Olivia walked into the kitchen.

The morning news crackled through the house:

Authorities tracked the violent bear throughout the night, finally catching and shooting him at the county line. Exhausted, the dog teams and hunters returned to their homes for a well-deserved rest.

Olivia ran back to the living room. The pictures showed their house from last night, several men riding ATVs, and a group of men laughing, slapping each other on the backs, and sitting around the dead bear. They held up Thunder's wobbly head by his ears.

Wildlife officials described the bear as a large male, around 25 years old. They could not explain its erratic and aggressive behavior. Doctor Rippledorn from the University told News 5 that Florida black bears are normally shy and retiring. He suggested that the drought earlier in the year may have driven this bear from its normal feeding patterns. Meanwhile, the Brophie and Corcoran children are safe at home, tired and bruised, but none the worse for their adventure. Coming up next, Alexis Alvarez with your weekend weather, and a community center is bringing more than free meals and after-school programs to local children.

"No. No! It isn't fair. He saved us. Those stupid rednecks killed him for no reason," Olivia screamed.

"I'm sorry Olivia," Uncle said. "Come on. Let's go get your breakfast."

"I don't want any breakfast." She slammed her hands down. "They think Thunder kidnapped us and it isn't true. They killed him!" Tears were streaming down her face.

"Thunder?"

"It . . . it's his name."

"You named him?"

"He helped us. He didn't hurt us at all. How come no one wonders why we weren't hurt if he is so dangerous?" she yelled, blasting her bedroom door shut.

The rest of the week was a blur. Olivia left several messages to her dad. She sat outside and watched the ancient walkingsticks come and go from the church up to the trees. It occurred to her that Squirt and the others must have made all of the white sand out here. Maybe all of the sand at the beach too.

She went into town with Aunt to get groceries. Aunt was strangely quiet in the car, always looking at her through the corner of her eyes. It felt like she was in trouble. Like she had to apologize for getting lost. Once, they stopped by the library so Aunt could go to her book club. Olivia saw Doug's mother hurry him out the side door.

One night, Olivia waited for the coral snakes to come home. She left them little piles of blueberries. She was going to prove, once and for all, that the corals were taking the berries. As they slithered by during sunset, she stood as close and as still as she could. Aunt stuck her head out the door, whispering as loudly as possible, "Olivia! Olivia! Get away from those snakes!" And in the time it took for her to turn her head and shush her, the corals had slithered off with all the berries.

Cheeto never left her side. He even went to bed early with her. Every night, she could hear the TV muffled through the walls. Before she knew it, Uncle would say goodnight from the hallway and the house would go silent. Tonight, she heard static coming from the closet and a faint whisper: "Olivia. Olivia. Can you hear me?"

Olivia snuck across her floor so the boards wouldn't creak and opened the closet. The backpack sat on the floor. The walkie-talkie! She grabbed it. "Doug? Is that you?"

"Yeah, I'm at home."

"Did you see the news? They killed Thunder."

"I know."

"I know. It isn't right. Poor thing. I'm going to find those jerks."

"Are you all right? I'm grounded. Mom doesn't want me to hang around you anymore. This was the first chance I got to call you."

"We can't leave the yard either. Aunt and Uncle are being nice to us. They think we were trying to run away. They're sending Gnat and me to summer school."

"No way. Well, I'll see you there. I'm going to get some extra credit."

"For what? You already get straight A's." Doug didn't answer.

"It was pretty cool in that cave. I was searching on the Internet and there is nothing out there about any of it. I wonder if we can get down in there again and take some pictures. You know, for evidence."

"Maybe. I think I'm going to call the TV news and tell them that the bear saved our lives."

"I gotta go. Call me later."

"See ya."

The house was silent. Olivia pulled the backpack out of the closet and took it back to bed. Under the covers, she unzipped the bag. A blue light burst under the sheets, filling the room with its glow. Back in the cave, when Gnat wasn't looking, she had stuffed the blue sphere into the backpack. Now, it was her secret. She hadn't even told Doug. She felt a little guilty stealing it from the chapel, but it was so smooth and warm in her hands. No one lived in that weird city anyway. No one would miss it.

Olivia stared into the sphere. The light throbbed, chimed, and hummed. Colors swirled around her fingers. She looked deep inside. It looked like ocean waves crashing and a burning sun all at the same time. It looked alive. She figured out that if she held her fingers just right against the smooth surface, the musical whispers coming from the sphere started to harmonize. She felt the chord align and deepen in her bones. It vibrated in her teeth and skull. It seemed so loud that she wondered if Aunt and Uncle were going to jump through the door wondering what the ruckus was about. But they didn't.

She pushed her fingers hard. The tones changed. It rolled in her hands. She pressed her cheek against its glassy surface. And then, pushing on a particularly tender note that was Olivia's favorite, a slice of the sphere shifted, sliding open as if on a hinge. The inside looked completely different from the outside. It was complicated, kind of like the inside of a clock. It wasn't exactly like a machine, but it moved as if there were gears and springs and a motor inside. Olivia couldn't see how it worked. She put her finger inside and flipped a red pedal to the right. The sphere unfolded a little bit more. Each of the little parts inside seemed to be made of a different material, a different element or substance. Olivia turned a particularly beautiful knob made of quartz. The color suddenly shifted to greenish-blue, like a tropical beach, and then to spinning red. The music started roaring. It wasn't even music anymore. It hurt her ears. It rattled and screamed. Still, no one came to the door. A screeching came, like the noise she heard at the paper mill in Portage. And then a chill ran down her skin. It was the same noise she heard when the Bobwhite Witch was staring at her in the woods. She quickly slid the sphere back together again and reared around to look at the window. There was no one there. With the sphere back together properly, blue light bathed her room once again. What it lit up was unmistakable.

The frogs had written another sentence in the dew. Olivia grabbed the *Learn Arabic* book and flipped frantically through the pages. It took her awhile, but she found the translation. For the next three nights, every night, Olivia practiced opening the sphere and the frogs wrote the exact same message on the glass. It said, "NOW YOU'VE DONE IT."

12

Cult of Wardenclyffe

The next night, Uncle snuck Olivia off into the living room as Gnat sat transfixed by the wavy images on the television. Somewhere in all of that static, a cartoon frog was breaking glasses by singing opera. Just the thought of that singing frog was enough to keep Gnat occupied the rest of the night. Aunt was in her sewing room crocheting an enormous slipcover for the TV. She "didn't appreciate the look of that ghastly thing."

Uncle took Olivia by the elbow and whispered, "I never finished my story. Follow me." He was so serious and intent, Olivia couldn't protest. They settled into a big brown chair, big enough for both of them. The giant opal boulder loomed over them. Olivia propped her feet up on its smooth edges.

From his pocket, Uncle pulled out a strange object. It appeared to be made of copper or brass. It looked like something a sailor would use to navigate the seas before radar was invented. In its center, a small wheel-like contraption spun and rotated whenever Uncle's hand moved in the slightest.

"This," Uncle said proudly, "is the only known Teslatron."

Olivia took it in her hands. The little wheel spun crazily. There were tiny numbers etched into the metal edges.

"For years," Uncle began, "I tried to figure out how it worked. I attended any lecture on electromagnetics that I could find at the universities. I read hundreds of books. Every once in a while, I would find another note from Nikola in a book I was reading. He had died years ago, but somehow he knew what I was going to be reading before I did.

"In one book, I found an ancient shred of parchment. It was a half-burnt page from *On Sphere-Making* by ancient Greece's greatest genius, Archimedes. Thousands of years ago, there was only one remaining copy of his famous book and it was held in the greatest library of all time, the Royal Library of Alexandria. The Royal Library was magnificent. All of the greatest thinkers, artists, mathematicians, alchemists, and poets of the time met there. It contained thousands of unique, one-of-a-kind texts. *On Sphere-Making* was the rarest and most important book in the entire library.

"In his office, deep inside the heart of the library, the Pappus of Alexandria worked day and night translating Archimedes' complicated and brilliant book. Armed guards protected his every move. He would not even allow anyone else on the same floor. The Pappus became more and more obsessed with his translations. He stopped eating. He grew pale and weak. Rumors swirled that he was possessed by the Crocodile King. But before he solved its secrets, before he understood the meaning of Archimedes' greatest work, Julius Caesar attacked Alexandria with his huge armies and completely destroyed the Royal Library. All of the scrolls and parchments were burned into ashes. The accumulated knowledge of the ancient world was gone and, along with it, Archimedes' book. The Pappus was found dead amongst the rubble, gripping what was left of a few, precious pages. Nikola left me the last remaining shred.

"The official story was that Archimedes' book was about manufacturing planetary models. But the parchment fragment proved that *On Sphere-Making* was actually a map. Not a map to help travelers find a particular place. But a map on how to find some *thing,* something of inexplicable value."

Uncle paused for effect. The candlelight shimmered across his face.

"What was it? What was so valuable?" Olivia asked.

"It is a map for finding the sphere, a machine that explains the true laws of the universe." Uncle paused. Then he went on.

"Nikola left other notes in other books too. All of them were clues, pieces of the puzzle that will ultimately lead to the sphere: a detailed description of the Omphalos of Delphi, a page from the apocryphal texts of the Bible describing the Tree of Knowledge, a diagram of the Antikythera and the Axis Mundi . . ."

"The huh?" Olivia was trying to keep up.

"Ummm . . . let me back up, slow down."

"Good idea," Olivia said, rolling her eyes.

"Throughout the history of man, we have been searching for answers. Answers to how the universe works, why we are here. Scientists, priests, physicists, mystics. All of them have been trying to answer the same questions. And it never seems like we get it right. We discover one thing and then another scientist comes along and proves it wrong. Over and over it has been like this, for thousands of years.

"Legends arose of a sphere. It was said to contain all of the answers. It is an encyclopedia with all of the scientific and spiritual answers. Does God exist? Are there parallel universes? Can we travel in time? What is the nature of light? How did life begin? Do we have souls? All of the important questions."

"Will it tell me where my Dad is?" Olivia asked.

"Well, I suppose it might. No one really knows what it really is or how it works. No one has ever found it. It is said that even if you do find it, making it work and deciphering it is impossible. It has moving parts and supposedly unfolds. But, like I said, no one really knows. Even those few unfortunate men who actually started getting close to the sphere . . ." His voice trailed off.

"What? Why are they so unfortunate?" Olivia perked up when she heard about the moving parts.

"Olivia," Uncle lowered his voice, "there are evil forces in the world that want the sphere and its secrets. As much as some people want it to be found and used for good, others want it to use it for evil. The Cult of Wardenclyffe was formed thousands of years ago to find the sphere and control its great power. They ravage through the world searching for the sphere and anyone that knows anything about it. These people are devious and tricky. They will do *anything* to get their hands on it. Conspiracies, wars, spies, collusion, assassins. It doesn't matter what they destroy or who they hurt. For years, they will be your friend, then POW, they get ya! As soon as someone starts getting close, starts figuring it all out, they are murdered and all of their research is taken. It happened to Nikola. It happened to the Pappus of Alexandria."

"Well, then why look for it? It sounds dangerous." Olivia was starting to worry.

"Good people *have* to look for it, Olivia. Good people have to find it before the bad people do." Uncle was staring very hard at her.

"Do you think Nikola had a map to find the sphere?"

"I don't know. I don't think so. But I do think he developed a way to find the sphere without the map. I think the sphere is at the third pole. I mean, I think the third pole follows the sphere wherever it goes. Tesla's seeds that I planted at the North and South Poles work together with the Teslatron to locate the sphere. I can't figure out how the Teslatron really works. It seems to be sensitive to the seed particles. But I can only tune it for a wide range. I've been all over these woods searching for a clue. I know it is here somewhere. Even if I could find the sphere, I have no idea how to work it. It is said that only a few special people can even figure it out." Uncle's face suddenly grew dark. "Don't you go blabbing this around town. And whatever you do, don't you go telling your aunt I told you."

"I w . . . w . . . won't tell," Olivia stuttered.

"After Nikola died, another man started working on the map. His name was Frank Lloyd Wright. He was a famous architect who lived in Wisconsin, not far from Sun Prairie."

"Hey! I know him! My class went to his house once."

"Taliesin. That is what he named it. His students officially learned how to design houses and buildings. But certain gifted students were also unlocking the secrets of the sphere map. In order to protect the map from the Cult of Wardenclyffe, Wright decided to burn everything that was ever learned and written about the map. He encoded that knowledge in a giant mural for a public garden called Midway Gardens, in downtown Chicago. The mural was a beautiful mosaic of multi-colored interlocking circles. The entire world loved his creation, but only Wright understood its true meaning. It was a code illustrating the known elements of the sphere map. It was very incomplete, mind you. He built the mural in a public garden so it couldn't be destroyed. He figured that a public mural would be the last place anyone would look for it. He also felt that it would help future scholars combat the powerful Cult. But the Cult of Wardenclyffe was furious when they learned that the map had been burned. While Wright was in Chicago finishing the mural, they killed his family and friends and burned Taliesin down.

"Wright was heartbroken. He built security guards to protect the mural. He called them Maid-in-the-Mud sprites. They looked like they were made from concrete, but if anyone tried to steal the mural, the sprites would come to life and destroy the thieves. The sprites also generated a photonic field between them, rendering cameras useless. That is why there are no existing photographs of the mural. He felt that the map would be safe with the sprites surrounding it.

"Years passed. Wright rebuilt Taliesin. He started his own chapter of the Fellowship to protect his secret research. The Fellowship had existed for eons in one form or another to combat the forces of Wardenclyffe. The Pappus of Alexandria was a member. Archimedes too. It was the only way that the map could be protected from the evil Cult. Members of the Fellowship are always in danger. Because of that, the Fellowship is very disorganized and scattered. You see, evil people will stop at nothing to get their way. Good people have boundaries. They never resort to the kind of tactics that allow the Cult to wage such violence and destruction. No one really knows how much of the map the Cult even possesses." Uncle paused and stared for a bit.

"Midway Gardens was bulldozed and turned into a breakwater on Lake Michigan. Not even the sprites could stop a fleet of bulldozers. The mural and its hidden map, the buildings, and the sprites, were all broken up and turned into landfill. Imagine that! America's greatest architect, and they bulldozed it just like that. Since there is no known picture of the actual mural, we have no idea what it said. Wright wrote down what he remembered on a single sheet of paper and disappeared for a while. Wardenclyffe burned down Taliesin a second time."

"Are you in the Fellowship?" Olivia asked.

"Oh, of course not!" Uncle answered. "I don't think the Fellowship even exists anymore, after what happened at Midway."

"Where is the map now?" Her hands were shaking as she spoke. She tried to act normal so Uncle wouldn't think anything wrong. She could barely keep her mind on the story, but she wanted to hear what happened.

"Wright was friends with a woman named Marjorie Kinnan Rawlings. They met at the University of Wisconsin, right up where you live. Wright told her everything he knew about the map. She followed his directions to central Florida. She moved here secretly during the night just after the second burning of Taliesin. She didn't even tell the other members of the Fellowship. I believe she was the last known living person to know the proximity of the sphere. She traveled all over Florida searching, but she never found it. The sphere might be right under our noses now, but it might be in France, or Australia. Who knows?"

"How does the sphere map work?" Olivia was confused.

Uncle laughed. "If I knew, I'd have the sphere. Nobody knows how it works, remember?"

"Oh, yeah." Olivia blushed.

"Besides, Nikola developed a better way to find it."

Uncle shrugged. "Because she never told anyone, Rawlings died of old age with her secrets intact. She had no notes or research. She was so smart, she kept it all in her head. She simply believed that the world's mysteries should remain mysteries. Now once again, no one, or no *thing*, knows where the sphere is hidden."

"Yeah. No one knows," Olivia said. "Um . . . do you know what it looks like? The sphere, I mean."

"It is supposed to be beautiful. Blue and green. Filled with color and music. Supposedly, the interior workings are intricately constructed from all of the elements, all of the critical substances that created the universe."

"Maybe you can show me how the Teslatron works. Maybe I can help you find it." Olivia was trying to act stupid. Her heart was pounding so hard she couldn't believe Uncle didn't notice.

"All these years, I've been trying to find it with the Teslatron." Uncle stared at his own hands. "But the stories say that only the Guardian will find the sphere. The Guardian and the sphere are drawn together by life events, by the very forces of nature. I believe that the telluric currents pull the Guardian to the sphere. The Guardian must have some special innate ability to follow the currents like a canoe on the river. It is as if the whole world, no, *the entire universe,* wants the Guardian to be in a certain place at a certain time to protect it. This is the way the sphere keeps getting moved and hidden. Whenever someone gets close, a Guardian appears and moves it someplace else. There is only one Guardian in the universe at a time and Wardenclyffe spies are always looking for him. They know that he will eventually lead them to the sphere, even if it is by accident. But the Guardian answers to no one. He doesn't want anyone to find it, the Wardenclyffe or even the Fellowship." Uncle quietly stared at Olivia for a long time.

"Your aunt and I moved down here some ten years after Rawlings, once I figured out some of how the Teslatron works. I really, really thought it had something to do with the Bermuda Triangle. The telluric lines are just too dynamic to pinpoint where they converge into the third pole.

"I gave up searching years ago. There are a hundred questions for every answer. It is all just old scraps of parchment and whispers in the dark. They are just old stories that too many bored and lonely people believe."

"Everyone thought Midway was completely destroyed. But years later, a sprite was found in a Wisconsin corn field. The spirit of the Guardian survived." He paused with a twinkle in his eye. "That was the year your mother was born."

"Are you saying my mother is the Guardian?" Olivia was skeptical.

"I have one rule in life, Olivia." He paused for effect. "Always say 'yes' to the possibilities. Now, off to bed."

As Olivia walked toward her bedroom, it never occurred to her that Aunt was at least a half century older than her Mom if Uncle's story was true. There was no way they could be sisters. Olivia was too worried about the Cult of Wardenclyffe to think about the ages of her relatives. Or to sleep.

13

Summer School

Olivia opened her door and yelled out into the house, "Can I wear shorts?"

"Yes, dear," Aunt replied.

"OK," she disappeared for a few moments before opening the door again. "Can I wear flip flops?"

"Of course."

"OK." She rummaged around in her closet.

"Hurry up! I don't want you to be late on your first day!" Olivia could hear a great ruckus of dishes and cabinet doors slamming in the kitchen. Cheeto ran out and barked at Aunt. Aunt was visibly upset that her own dog seemed to be against her now, ever since the kids had run away into the woods.

Olivia and Gnat stood at the end of the long, overgrown, crooked, sandy driveway. They didn't have to wait long. They could hear the squeaking brakes of the bus before they could see it. Soon, a royal blue bus with one white stripe drove into view.

"Blue?" Olivia pondered. "Blue?"

"Good morning, Miss Olivia." The bus driver smiled as he opened the creaking door. "Good morning Gnat."

"Good morning, Mr. Transportation," Gnat piped.

The bus driver chuckled. "You can call me Mr. Ott," he said, gruffly closing the door.

Olivia didn't even bother to question how a complete stranger might know her name. She grabbed Gnat's hand and made her way to the back seat. No one was sitting back there. There were only four kids on the bus. Doug was one of them, sitting halfway back. As she passed, she said, "Come on."

"To the back!" Gnat was so excited to be going to school for *enrichment* he was exploding with glee.

Doug stood up, protesting. "Olivia!" he whispered. "Olivia! Cuke and the Mutches are the next stop!" But she kept on walking. She acted like she couldn't hear him. She plopped down in the very back seat. Olivia opened her window as the bus started moving.

"Miss Olivia!" Mr. Ott scolded, and then realized that he sounded too angry. "Please sit down and close your window. The air conditioner on this thing hardly works." As he looked in his mirror, all he could really see were three kids in the back seat whispering excitedly together. He knew she was a celebrity in Lyonia now. Everyone had seen her on the national news. But he also knew he didn't want any trouble, and there was something troubling about her. He had decided this morning to be as polite to her as possible although no other child on the bus would *ever* think of him as polite.

"Look what I found," Doug said, pulling a large book out of his backpack and starting to flip through the pages. "I knew I'd seen a picture of them before."

"Of who? Picture of who?"

"Here," he said, handing the book over to her. There was a big picture of a sea urchin fossil. The caption read, "Fossilized echinoderm. Cambrian era. 8 cm."

"It's Squirt. You found him!"

"It says they went extinct millions of years ago. They are related to starfish and sand dollars."

"Well, they aren't extinct anymore."

"I suppose not."

"Plus they eat candy," Gnat added.

Before long, the bus stopped again. The Mutches stomped up the stairs and knocked the first lunch box they saw onto the floor. Cuke was the first to see Olivia, Doug, and Gnat sitting in their seat. He punched both of the twins and pointed back at them.

"Oh, here we go," Doug whispered. But to his surprise, they simply turned around and sat up front near the bus driver. "Why are they sitting up there?"

"Who cares?" Gnat said. Some of the younger kids moved back a few seats to get some distance between themselves and the bullies.

"Well, it sounds like everything the scientists think is wrong. I'll bet none of scientists even know they make sand, huh?"

"Yeah, I forgot about that," Doug said with a faraway look.

Cuke kept turning around and looking at them in the back seat. When Olivia turned to the window, Cuke shook his fist at Doug.

"Listen. I still have to tell you. Back in the cave. You know, the cave we were lost in?" Doug asked.

"Ummmm . . . yeah." Olivia laughed. "I think I remember something like that."

"Well, remember the tardigrade? I didn't just ride it. I talked to it. I mean, I commanded it. Like a dog. And it did whatever I said. Except I didn't even know what I was saying."

"Huh?" Gnat was playing his video game.

"I spoke in a language I don't even know."

"What language?" asked Olivia.

"That's just it. I don't know."

"Well, say something in it. Tell me 'Hi, my name is Doug.' Maybe I can figure it out. My last teacher was from Columbia. Maybe I can tell what it is."

"I doubt it was Columbian."

"Say 'Hi, my name is Doug,'" she repeated.

"Say 'I'm a stinking acorn chucker,'" Gnat said without looking up.

"No. You guys!" Doug shoved Gnat. "I can't. I mean, I've tried. All week I've been trying to speak it again and all that comes out is blah blah blah."

"Blah blah blah?"

"Yeah. Gibber jabber. But in the cave, I just knew it. It just came out of me."

"Maybe you were just lucky. Maybe you were crying and the tardigrade felt bad."

"I wasn't crying!" Doug slammed his book into his backpack and stared at his feet. Soon, the bus turned off the road and pulled into Silver Boils Elementary. Olivia liked the palm trees in the front.

"Silver Boils?" Olivia thought. "What kind of name is that?" A cheerful-looking woman was waiting for her as she stepped off the bus.

"Olivia?" Her voice was incredibly squeaky and she had a thick Southern accent. "You must be Olivia Brophie. And you must be Nathan." She roughed up Gnat's hair. "I'm Mrs. Vitaly. Please come with me. I need to check you in."

"Uh, hi." Olivia was suddenly very nervous about this new school.

"You two are probably wondering all about Silver Boils Elementary, aren't you?" She stopped walking as she waited for an answer.

"Uh, yeah." Olivia wasn't really interested, but it seemed like Mrs. Vitaly really wanted to tell the story. Olivia and Gnat had to jog to keep up with her.

"Silver Boils is named for the small sulphur springs that boil up from the ground." Mrs. Vitaly raised her arms upward, simulating how she thought the water emerged. Gnat scrunched his nose. "You can see the boils down there behind the swing set next to the woods. For decades it was used by ranchers to water their cattle. It was the only water source for twenty miles. Ranchers started fighting for rights to the water. A great feud erupted, threatening to tear the county apart," Mrs. Vitaly bustled through the front doors of the school. Olivia watched Doug shuffle off down the hall. "This way, sugar," she said, pulling Olivia the other direction. "Fearing the start of a war, the brilliant founders of Lyonia bought the land even though it was far distant from the town's borders during that time. Lyonia suddenly became the largest town in Catkin County, even though it had the smallest population. War was averted. The boils were available to every rancher free of charge. Silver Boils became forever known throughout the land as a place of peace and reconciliation."

Olivia smiled to herself. Mrs. Vitaly's enthusiasm was catching as her squeaky Southern accent rang through the halls. There weren't many kids in the school, but they were all watching her and Gnat. Whenever Olivia looked toward them, they turned away and whispered. Hundreds of construction paper kites hung with yarn from the ceiling, twisting in the breeze as they rushed by.

"Right this way please," Mrs. Vitaly continued as they sped into her office. "As you are aware, Nathan, your teacher this summer will be Mrs. Bartow. And Olivia, your teacher will be Miss Rinkle." The kids stared blankly at her. "You do know that, right?"

"No one told us," Olivia said, examining the multitude of certificates on the wall. State Historical Society honorary member. School Board Advisory Committee. Catkin County Vice Principal of the Month: September 1994. Successful Completion of Beginning Computers Certificate. Lyonia Citizen of the Year: 2007. A picture of Mrs. Vitaly shaking the hand of some man in a suit.

"Oh dear. Well, I suppose you only just signed up last week. You should consider yourself lucky to even be here today. It is a miracle in itself that I have been able to single-handedly maintain the Silver Boils' tradition of excellent academic summertime programs. It hasn't exactly been easy during these times of budget scarcity. It was a stroke of subtle genius inviting the entire School Board to my home for spring cotillion." Mrs. Vitaly paused for a moment with a small smile before resuming. "No bother. You are already on the class rosters and your teachers are expecting you. I certainly hope that you fulfilled your checklist . . . correct?"

"Umm . . ."

"Your supplies? Your school supply checklist?" Olivia opened her bag and removed one notebook and three pencils. Mrs. Vitaly stood straight up. "Come with me," she ordered, brushing past them. "It is a good thing for you that I have memorized the checklists of every teacher in my jurisdiction," she said, opening up a closet. Inside, the shelves overflowed with lost and abandoned supplies that she had collected over the years.

"Open your bags." A flurry of supplies started flying off the shelves and into Olivia's and Gnat's bags. "That should do although you might want to check the highlighters and glue sticks to make sure they haven't run dry. Please make every attempt to replace the supplies that I have given you. Supplies don't grow out of thin air. Now, I see that I have your health certificates. We are still waiting for your marks from . . . let's see . . . . yes, Sun Prairie. Well, I can't give you credit until I receive your marks. Here is a list of our rules and regulations. I won't expect you to know them today. Aren't you a dear?" she said, gleaming at Gnat.

"I'm an alien assassin," he responded confidently.

"Oh my! That's a big word for your age!" The bell rang. "Well, let's be off then. I'll show you to your classrooms. Because it is summer school, we have to combine some grades together. That is not an excuse for misbehavior. I don't tolerate misbehavior at Silver Boils," she said, gripping Olivia's shoulder a little tighter.

They walked back out into the hallway where it was suddenly very quiet. All of the lights were off. "Silver Boils is a pilot school for environmental stewardship." Mrs. Vitaly glowed. "We are carbon neutral! That is why when the bell rings, the lights in the hallway turn off thirty seconds later. You will get used to it. Ah, here we are, Nathan. Mrs. Bartow's room."

"Bye, Gnat. I'll meet you at the bus after school," Olivia said.

"Adios," he replied shuffling into the class room. Olivia heard applause exploding in the room as she and Mrs. Vitaly walked farther down the dark hallway.

"Olivia, now that we are alone, I have to ask you . . ." Mrs. Vitaly paused. "Will they . . . I mean, do *they* follow you everywhere you go?"

"Huh? I don't understand. Who?"

"The bears. I have to look out for the safety of all of the children. We can't have bears lounging about in the playground."

"What are you talking about?" Olivia started to panic.

Suddenly flustered, Mrs. Vitaly pushed her into Miss Rinkle's classroom. "Never mind, sugar. We will elucidate the subject later." And before Olivia could ask her what "elucidate" meant, the door closed behind her.

Olivia turned around to face a room full of silent, wide-eyed children from three grade-levels watching her every move. At the front of the class was a young woman waving a very long, twisted stick.

14

The Bear Charmer

"Good morning, Olivia. What kind of stick do you suppose this is?" Miss Rinkle pointed the twisted branch at her.

"Uh . . . I don't . . . I don't know." Her voice faded. She could see the Mutch twins, Cuke, and Begonia snickering in the back of the room. It figured that all four of them would be in summer school. All twenty-three kids in class watched to see what was going to happen next.

"It is important in life, children, to understand the world in which you live. Every day I see people who have no idea what is going on around them. They live in a fog, going to work, rushing home to turn on the TV. They do not appreciate the beautiful world that is right under their noses." Olivia was starting to blush. "Any guesses, Miss Olivia?"

"It's a . . . um . . . a vomiting holly?" she stammered the only name of a tree she could remember. The entire room erupted with laughter.

"What an interesting answer. You may take your seat, Olivia," said Miss Rinkle, pointing the stick to an open desk. Olivia slumped toward her seat. She saw that it was on the opposite side of the room from Doug. "These are to be your assigned desks for the summer." Miss Rinkle paused, looking around the room. "Cucumber! That is your name correct? Cucumber? You seem to think this is funny. What kind of stick do you think this is?"

"Errrrr. . . . my mom won't let me outside on account of my allergies," he lied, shifting in his seat.

"That is no reason to be ignorant of nature, Mr. Cucumber. Anyone else?" The class was silent. Someone dropped a pen onto the floor. "Let's try this. Who can find a word to describe this stick?"

"Wood?" Richard Mutch shouted out, thinking it was funny to state the obvious.

"Why yes, it is wood! What else?"

"Bark . . . y?" a girl in the corner offered. The class giggled and she blushed. But Miss Rinkle didn't laugh.

"Yes, it has bark. It is weird bark though, isn't it? It is thin and shreddy. Who else? Douglas?"

"It is . . . crooked," Doug said.

"Yes! It is indeed crooked. That is its name, the crooked-wood tree. Doug and Richard, good job! Does anyone know the scientific name for the crooked-wood tree?"

Olivia couldn't believe that Miss Rinkle would ask a question like that. How were they supposed to know? What grade did she think this was?

"The official, scientific name of crooked-wood is. . . . Lyonia. That's right. Our town is named after this tree." Miss Rinkle surveyed the class triumphantly. Her gray eyes pierced the room. Her shining caramel-colored hair flowed to her shoulders. "This summer, we are going to learn all of the trees in the woods out back. And the animals too. We are going to learn to pay attention to the world around us."

Olivia glanced over at Doug who looked like he was breathing a sigh of relief. "He's going to ace it," Olivia thought.

"And we are also going to spend some time on geometry." Olivia noticed that Doug tensed up again. "For the rest of the morning, let's just talk about who we are, our interests, and our plans for the summer. Because this afternoon, we have a series of evaluations in every subject so we know what we need to work on." The class exploded again. "I know, I know. No one wants to take a test, especially on the first day of summer school. But look at it this way. If everyone does well on a subject, we don't have to spend time studying it and we can take more field trips."

By lunchtime, Olivia actually liked Miss Rinkle. She seemed to really care about teaching. She appeared to be interested in what they were saying. And on top of it, she definitely seemed to enjoy picking on the bullies.

In the cafeteria, a crowd of little kids circled around Gnat. They were laughing and patting him on his back. Over by the windows, she saw Larry Mutch shove Doug into the wall. "Is she still your girlfriend?" he sneered.

Cuke was hopping around like a goat yelling, "Git 'em! Git 'em!"

"Hey!" Olivia yelled across the cafeteria. "Leave him alone!" Larry and Cuke turned around. Realizing who was yelling, they scrambled away, but not before shoving Doug one more time.

"What is their problem?" she said on reaching Doug. He was trying to put his notebook back in order.

"Nothing. They're always like that."

"What were they saying? They were saying something."

"Never mind. Let's eat. It's Salisbury steak day. It's the only good food they make here. I found some stuff on tardigrades."

"Why are they so scared of me?"

"Look. Everyone is saying that you . . . that you are in with the bears. Mr. Mutch drives a tow truck and he says that he sees bears in your yard at night. Like they are protecting your house. Well, they say you sleep among them out in the woods."

Olivia's heart skipped a beat. "That can't be true. I haven't seen any bears. Not since Thunder anyway." Her mind was racing. She remembered what Mrs. Vitaly said earlier about keeping the students safe. "Why haven't I seen any?"

"It's just a rumor. It will stop." But even Doug had a worried look in his eyes.

"You don't think I attract bears, do you?" Olivia asked.

"No. No. It's just a rumor. It's probably from the news the other night."

"Hello, kids." It was Miss Rinkle. "Mind if I eat lunch with you? I love Salisbury steak."

Olivia wanted to say no. She had a million questions for Doug. But she knew she had to say yes. "Uh . . . OK," she answered.

"Yeah, sure," Doug replied.

"Are you feeling all right, Olivia? You look pale." She put her hand on Olivia's forehead.

"I'm fine, just hungry," she lied. She felt faint. Since that night they returned from the cave, she hadn't even gone into the woods. She only stood at the edge to watch the walkingsticks and corals. Aunt wouldn't let her out of her sight for fear she would run away again, and Uncle hadn't said anything about bears hanging around. Maybe Thunder came back! Maybe he wasn't dead after all! She couldn't wait to go home. All through lunch she barely heard anything Mrs. Rinkle said. She *did* hear Doug yammering on about tardigrades and mammoths. She kicked him under the table.

The afternoon was worse. Olivia noticed every little glance and whisper from the other kids. She couldn't concentrate on any of the tests. All of the little answer-circles on the test blended together. It took all of her concentration just to fill in the answers without marking outside the lines. She couldn't even remember a question after she answered it. She was sure she flunked them all. Time was dragging. The good news was that the school day was one hour shorter during summer than it was during the regular school year.

When the final bell sounded, Olivia was already on the blue bus before the ringing in her ears stopped. "Hi, Mr. Ott!" She sat in the front seat. Mr. Ott looked a little nervous. His eyes kept glancing at her in the mirror. Gnat was loitering in the school yard with his classmates. Olivia opened her window. "Gnat! Come on! It's time to go!"

The bus couldn't start fast enough. She was more than a little jealous that Gnat was making new friends so easily. She used to have friends at school. She was never *super* popular like Julia McNamara back in Sun Prairie. But no one actually hated her. Still, part of her liked how it felt when the Mutches sped past her seat on the bus, tripping on their own feet, not wanting to look her in the eyes. Part of her felt like maybe for once the bullies could be the ones to be a little scared. And maybe the other kids too. If they couldn't take the time to be nice to her, than that was *their* problem. Let them whisper and run the other way. A little smile curved across her lips.

Thankfully, the bus ride seemed short. She listened to Doug and Gnat bickering about who was the most afraid down in the cave. Next thing she knew, it was their stop. She flew out the door pulling Gnat behind her. Storming through the kitchen, she threw her books on the table and headed for the back door.

"Wait! How was your first day? Olivia!" Aunt called out to her.

"Just a second," she said as the door shut. She ran out to the backyard. She stepped quietly into the woods.

"Hello?" she peered into the thicket. "Is anyone there?" She listened. The forest was strangely quiet. Several steps into the trees, she looked down. There it was. Obvious in the sand. A bear track. In fact, there were lots of them. There were so many tracks they formed a trail through the bushes. The trail curved around as if the bears had been pacing a wide circle around the Milligans' house. She followed the tracks a few yards.

"Hello?" A leaf dropped from up in the trees and nestled down onto the sand. Somewhere a tree cricket trilled. A giant walkingstick watched her from the oaks, calmly munching a mouthful of foliage.

"Hello?" Olivia squinted into the shadows. "What do you want? Where are you? Thunder, is that you?" She couldn't see anything. Just bushes. And lots of white sand.

"Olivia! Come inside please," Aunt yelled out to her. "What are you doing out there anyway? You have company!"

Olivia looked around one more time and wandered back into the house. There, at her kitchen table, gray eyes sparkling in the afternoon air, sat Miss Rinkle.

15

Floating Away

"That's a lovely necklace," Miss Rinkle said, reaching out to Olivia's neck. "I've never seen beads like those." She grabbed the beads with her long fingers and slowly pulled Olivia closer. "Just lovely. Where did you buy them?"

Olivia paused. Miss Rinkle was so beautiful and sophisticated. She didn't think it would be such a good idea to tell her that coral snakes gave her the beads. She would probably think Olivia was some dumb country fool. "I . . . I found them."

"Miss Rinkle and I have been discussing your grades, Olivia," Aunt said, picking up the teacups and wanting to change the subject.

"Yes, Olivia. I graded your tests from this afternoon. How do you think you did?"

Olivia's mouth suddenly dried up. She couldn't speak.

Miss Rinkle's laughter rang like chimes through the house. "Olivia, you scored one hundred percent. I even gave you a test for eighth grade. You are the only child in the entire class that passed their grades, much less scored one hundred on an eighth grade test."

"What do you mean? Doug is smarter than I am." Her mind raced. How could that be?

"Olivia, I can't talk to you about another student's grades. But you are simply going to be bored in class this summer. I would like to spend an extra hour with you every day — here, in your home after school. I can give you special assignments. Like a private tutor! Would you like that?"

"I don't know," Olivia said, shuffling her feet. Cheeto was staring at Miss Rinkle and growling under his breath. "There's other stuff . . ."

"Now listen, Olivia." Aunt cut her off. She wasn't about to let another hour of free supervision pass by without a fight. One hour of tutoring is one less hour of running wild in the woods and showing up on the evening news. "You've been acting strangely ever since . . . well, ever since you were lost. You hardly ever come out of your room. . . . This is a great opportunity for you, dear. Don't you like Miss Rinkle?"

"Well, yes." Olivia's blood was starting to boil. Aunt didn't even know her before the past couple of weeks. How could she know who was acting strange and who wasn't?

"And don't you want to learn new things? Miss Rinkle is a trained biologist, you know."

"Olivia," Miss Rinkle spoke softly, holding her hand, "I'm new to Lyonia, just like you. I don't have any friends around here. I know how hard it is to move somewhere new." Miss Rinkle's eyes drew her in and calmed her. "I don't want to rush you. Think about it and let me know tomorrow." She raised a quick finger toward Aunt who was about to interject. Aunt closed her mouth.

"OK, we can," Olivia agreed after a long pause. Miss Rinkle smiled warmly. Aunt stepped back with a proud look on her face. She could almost feel the two women pull the answer out of her. It was the only answer they were willing to accept. Like a stubborn pony being pulled out of the paddock, Olivia obliged. Truthfully, she was dreading it. Miss

Rinkle was nice and sort of cool. It made her feel special. But she had a lot of things to do, not the least of which was figuring out what the blue sphere was and what was going on in the caves beneath Florida. She also had to figure out how to get her dad or mom on the phone.

"Good. I'll be over tomorrow at three p. m. sharp." Miss Rinkle grabbed her bag and started walking for the door. She was suddenly very eager to leave. Her eyes darted about the room, taking in all of the exotic decorations. The door shut behind her and a swirl of faint perfume hung in the hair. To Olivia, it smelled like freshly plowed corn fields.

That night, Olivia waited in her room until she was sure everyone in the house was asleep.

She had become good at opening the sphere. It worked best if she listened carefully to the noises coming out. She could tell if she was turning the wrong knob or opening the wrong door by the changing tones and volume. It helped if she didn't use her eyes too much either. There were switches and panels in there that looked tempting but were definitely the wrong thing to do. The sphere peeled open like a strange citrus fruit in her hands. Its gentle glow filled the room. Her fingers flickered over the sphere like spider legs. She could feel its energy surge through her.

And then, she saw it. A knob that looked like it was made of . . . of water! How can that be? Water! She touched it with her finger. It felt cool. There was a wet smudge on her finger where it had made contact. How can water, wet, drippy, sloppy water make a knob? Ice maybe. But water? Slowly, slowly, she reached in and turned the knob. The sphere went silent. For a second, nothing happened.

Olivia felt queasy. Her stomach turned. Her head reeled. And then she suddenly realized she was slowly rising up from her mattress. The sheets around her billowed like they were hung on a clothesline in the breeze. She looked over to her bookcase. It was lifting up from the floor. It was floating! Books tumbled and fell upwards. Flying! A moment of shock rushed through her. Everything in the room rose slowly upward. Even her legs left the mattress. She felt light as a dandelion seed. She swung her arms around to reach down and grab the sphere but her weightless body tumbled in the wrong direction. She ended up even farther away and higher up. The lamp from her nightstand bobbed up by the ceiling. Olivia concentrated. She swung her legs out behind her and grabbed a blanket that was still tucked under the mattress. She pulled herself down. Her legs kicked high above her head. She pushed the water switch inside the sphere back to its original position.

With an incredibly loud crash, everything in the room came slamming back to the ground. Olivia bounced off the mattress onto the floor. Her lamp shattered. Books scattered on the floor.

"What in the blazes was that?" She heard Uncle storming down the hallway. "Is everyone all right? Gnat?"

Olivia scrambled to reassemble the sphere. Just as she put the last piece in place and its blue glow faded, Uncle opened her door.

"Olivia, are you all . . . What happened in here?"

Olivia stared at him. "I . . . I . . . don't know. It just happened."

"Hmmmmm. Must have been a sonic boom. Sometimes the navy flies over here if there are storms offshore. Are you all right?"

Olivia nodded. Her hands were shaking so badly she couldn't believe that Uncle didn't notice.

"That was one big boom. The house is a disaster. I swear I bounced halfway to the ceiling!" he said in disbelief. Olivia mustered a half-hearted

laugh. "Well, let's get this cleaned up and you back to bed. Crisis is over."

"Uh, that's OK. I can do it." Olivia leapt out of bed and filled her arms with books. She didn't want Uncle to find the sphere by accident. "Maybe Gnat needs help."

"All right. Well, goodnight. Wake me up if you need anything."

Olivia could hear Uncle and Gnat in the next room for several minutes before the house went dark and quiet again. She let out a loud exhale.

She wouldn't learn until morning that the mess extended far from her bedroom. The weightlessness rippled out from the sphere, so she had the worst of it. Still, the morning news spoke of a "geostationary satellite" veering out of orbit. *Scientists were baffled. Weather reports will be less accurate until a replacement is launched. Electrical service was out in several rural communities across central Florida. A small earthquake may be to blame. Too weak to be felt, the quake probably centered on an old fault line in the middle of the Gulf of Mexico.*

That one, brief few seconds of no gravity had caused a mess!

When the bus rumbled down the road, Olivia was relieved to see it was still blue and still smelled like corn chips. She sank into her seat and breathed a sigh of relief.

16

Unmasking the Witch

Several weeks went by and Olivia really started to enjoy going to school. Miss Rinkle always asked her the hardest questions and none of the other kids gave her any problems. The best part of all was when Miss Rinkle would stop by after school for her private teaching. She learned all sorts of new things, mostly about history and science. But Miss Rinkle made all of it interesting. She taught with stories and Olivia would feel like she was really there, back with the Greeks or in the middle of the Battle of New Orleans. She taught her what life was like before the number zero was invented, and before television and radio. She learned what an amazement it was to the world when it was discovered that dirty water made people sick.

Whenever she had trouble with a question, Miss Rinkle would ask easier questions until she could figure out the harder ones. She never got mad or gave her a horrible score. She would just say how proud she was of her and one day, when she had a little girl of her own, she hoped she turned out just like Olivia.

On Mondays, Miss Rinkle would stand silently in front of the massive bookshelves in the Milligans' house. She called Uncle's bookshelves "eclectic" and "quite invigorating." Her eyes methodically scanned across each shelf. Olivia sat on the floor watching her. She could almost hear

Miss Rinkle thinking. Suddenly, she would remove a book and announce, "This is the one! You have until Friday to finish reading it." Miss Rinkle always picked a hard book, like *How to Build Your Own Laser* by Michael Wembley or *Travels* by William Bartram. Olivia never had a clue what that week's assignment was going to be. But it was her favorite part of the week. She could hardly wait for school to be over on Mondays so she could rush home and find out what grown-up book she would be assigned to read.

One morning in mid-July, Olivia walked into Silver Boils Elementary to find the entire classroom gathering by the school's back doors. A few seconds later, the younger class turned the corner led by Mrs. Bartow and joined the older kids. Gnat came over and stood with Olivia and Doug. All of the children were chattering loudly. Mrs. Vitaly's voice rose above the noise. "Children! Children! Calm down or there will be no field trip! Children!" Her plea for silence went unnoticed. Begonia punched Cuke so hard in the shoulder he stumbled in a heap of knees and elbows into the lockers. The un-twins yowled with glee. Minutes passed. Mrs. Vitaly fretted next to the drinking fountain.

After several chaotic minutes, down the dark hallway, a giant straw hat appeared. It reminded Olivia of a sombrero or something an old lady would wear in the garden. It made its way toward the children. About halfway, they could see the shape of the person wearing the hat. Olivia knew right away that it was Miss Rinkle because she was using the crooked wood as a walking stick. With every step closer, the chattering became quieter and quieter.

When Miss Rinkle made it to the front of the group, her face appeared out of the shadow of the hat and she raised her stick high into the air.

"If," she announced quietly, "we observe strict silence and maintain our lines, there is no telling what fantastic creatures we will see. If you choose to break the silence or wander off, we will all come back inside and take geometry tests this morning." She said it with such sincerity and authority, that the children immediately arranged themselves into three quiet lines. Mrs. Vitaly seemed a bit perturbed that order was so oddly and easily established by Miss Rinkle, but she nodded her head in her direction and scurried off down the hall to her office where she hoped to spend a quiet morning completing certification applications for the upcoming school year and filling out budget projections.

"Where do you think we are going?" Doug whispered to Olivia.

"Maybe we'll go see Squirt," Olivia said, laughing.

Miss Rinkle led the group of children out the back door, through the playground, and down a nature trail pointing her walking stick at various plants, birds, and butterflies. She knew more than just the names too. She knew the stories behind everything. She showed the kids what plants each insect liked to eat and how to use a bush to sneak up on a busy woodpecker.

Miss Rinkle turned her head to point out some hanging Spanish moss. "This hanging moss, children, is actually closely related to pineapples. Can you imagine pineapples hanging like this?" She laughed. "Actually, pineapples grow from the ground in tropical areas such as Hawaii. In olden times, settlers used hanging moss to stuff their mattresses and pillows. I wouldn't try that though, without cleaning and drying it thoroughly. The moss, you see, is filled with spiders and chiggers, among other small creatures. It would make for a very restless night. If you would like, later this summer, I will show you how to clean it and we can make pillows."

Olivia beamed with pride. Only Doug and Gnat knew that Miss Rinkle visited her after school, but she felt special. She wanted to be exactly like Miss Rinkle when she grew up. Every child listened to her stories, enraptured.

Almost every child.

Richard, Larry, Begonia, and Cuke were hatching a plan. They were very sneaky about it too. Over the years, they had learned how to appear like they were paying attention and behaving, but actually plotting for trouble. Just by glancing at each other, faking exaggerated yawns, and rolling their eyes, they came to a unanimous agreement.

"Oh!" Miss Rinkle exclaimed, rushing over to a small cactus. "Children come close. Do you see this little bit of cotton growing on this cactus?" She gently removed the bit of cotton with her fingernail. "This is the house of the cochineal insect. Now watch closely." Ever so softly, she squeezed the tiny insect inside the cotton. A single drop of bright red liquid squirted out onto her finger. Some of the girls squealed. "The cochineal was once the finest red dye that money could buy and it was grown on sacred Aztec farms. The Spanish hoarded its secret because it was worth its weight in gold. People lost their lives trying to acquire its riches." Carefully, she placed the bit of cotton back on the cactus. "There you go, little gem," she chimed.

As she spoke, the four bullies stepped backwards together in unison, never turning their backs on the watchful teacher. Before long, they had worked their way from the front of the line to the back. Within ten minutes, the boys were all in line behind Doug and Gnat. Begonia stayed directly in front of Olivia.

"So, Dougie, are you married to Milligan yet?" Cuke snickered under his breath.

"Leave us alone, Cuke," Olivia shot back. "Can't you just get a life?"

"Milligan, you ain't all that." Begonia turned around. They were surrounded. The rest of the class disappeared around the curving trail up ahead. There was nothing but trees and bullies. "You been walkin' around like you own the place, Milligan. We ain't gonna let you make fools of us no more."

It was the most Olivia ever heard Begonia say. Richard had his arm wrapped around Doug's neck. She couldn't really see a way out of this one.

"Gnat, run!" she yelled. But Cuke grabbed his backpack and shoved him to the ground. And then Olivia said it. She didn't really mean to, it just slipped out. It was the worst thing she could possibly have said at that moment. "Everyone knows you two are not twins and that your Daddy just put you in the same grade because one of you is too dumb and the other is too slow!" A moment of hush came over the bullies. No one had ever said such a thing. Begonia looked at Larry and Richard. Cuke relaxed his grip on Gnat just a little bit. Richard looked shocked. Larry's face turned bright purple.

"It was you bustin' up on our traps, wasn't it? You sure you ain't a witch too, Milligan? Just like your aunt." Larry sneered. Richard started slapping the back of Doug's head so hard tears welled up in his eyes. Rage, along with fear, built up in Olivia like never before. Even in the cave she was not so scared, but she pushed her fear down. Her hands curled into fists and she lunged like lightning at Begonia. She hit her as hard as she could, right in the stomach. She looked up, expecting to see Begonia wince in pain. She only laughed.

Begonia punched back.

Olivia hit the ground. She could barely breathe. She had never been punched before. It surprised her how much it actually hurt. But she jumped up swinging. She was able to land one punch on Richard's nose. Blood was everywhere as he let out a yelp. Doug fell to the ground when Larry punched him in the stomach. His papers were blowing all around into the bushes. It was only Olivia and four big bullies now. She didn't stand a chance. Begonia was smacking her in the face and laughing.

Suddenly, the trees behind them exploded with a violent crash. A bear, bristling with rage, jumped out onto the trail and pushed Begonia down with his heavy shoulder. Begonia flew backwards to the ground, cutting her ear on a stump. She scrambled to her feet and ran up the trail screaming, "Bear! Bear!" The un-twins and Cuke stood frozen. The bear stood bristling between them and Olivia. He stepped forward, baring his teeth. All three of them instantly wet their pants. Olivia started laughing. Richard saw her laughing and started to cry.

"Go on! Get out of here!" she yelled at the bullies. "If you bother me again, it's going to be a lot worse for you!" They scrambled as fast as they could back toward school. Cuke's sneaker sat by itself on the trail behind him. Olivia spun around like a ballerina and jumped up in the air laughing. "That's what you get!" she yelled some more at the bullies. "That's what you will all get! And I'm not a Milligan. I'm a Brophie!" She hugged the bear around the neck and said, "Thank you, sweetie. I'll be fine. Now go." To her surprise, the bear did just that.

Doug sat on the ground. He looked at her with a different face. He looked afraid of her. "Doug, come on. Get up."

"I can get up myself. Don't touch me!" he screamed.

"Doug, it's me. It's all right! They're gone."

"I . . . I know. I just don't want . . . I can get up by myself." Doug was more than a little embarrassed. Not only was he beat up by Richard, but now Olivia really *was* a bear charmer. He had known it deep down inside. It started back when that big bear brought them a loaf of bread and she acted like it was all normal. Now he couldn't deny it. Part of him wished he never got caught up with Olivia to begin with. He started picking up all of his papers and shoving them into his bag.

"Are you OK, Gnat?" Olivia asked. He was crying and rubbing his elbow.

None of them saw that, just down the trail, Miss Rinkle had been standing and watching the entire episode. She turned and hustled the class back to the school building.

This trip to Mrs. Vitaly's office felt quite a bit different than the first day of summer school. Olivia sat alone in her office while Mrs. Vitaly stood outside whispering to Miss Rinkle. It didn't take a genius to figure out what they were discussing. Olivia had never heard such grave and ominous whispers.

"Olivia," Mrs. Vitaly said sternly as she bustled into her office, "if it were just up to myself, you would be expelled right at this moment."

"But . . ."

"No buts about it," Mrs. Vitaly interrupted. Her thick Southern accent had taken on a disturbingly dark tone. "You represent a danger to the children and to the sterling reputation of Silver Boils." She paused. "This just won't do. You also represent a situation in which there is no precedent. Imagine the phone calls that I have to make this afternoon, Olivia. Can you fathom my discussion with Mr. Mutch or Mrs. Salt? Oh Lord. The Board!" she glanced at her certificates on the wall. "They will go unhitched when they find out that I am not going to expel you. Do you know that every single member of the Board came out to your house to help search for you? And most of them helped hunt down that bear. So you cannot argue that they do not care about your unfortunate . . . situation."

"But Larry . . ." Olivia felt bad, but Mrs. Vitaly was blaming the wrong person. The thought of another bear getting shot sent an angry chill down her skin.

"Now listen, I know all about those bullies. Those four have been exacerbating their relationships with the other children for years. That is why they are in summer school to begin with, Olivia. All of these children need the extra classroom experience in order to keep up with their classmates. Order and scholastic dedication are so critical during the summer months. Only you and Nathan are here on holiday, to pass the time. We made special accommodations for you. Furthermore, think about Doug and his safety."

"Doug is smarter than I am," Olivia blurted out. "He knows all that stuff Miss Rinkle was showing us out there. He even knows scientific names. He just won't say it because of those bullies!"

"Doug Corcoran is a fine young man. And he is smart. Very smart. But since his father died . . . his mother just can't do everything. Doug is flunking all of his subjects. He needs to focus on his studies. If he is not careful, he will be held back. He needs some peace and quiet so he can figure things out. It is time you consider that." Mrs. Vitaly sounded like she blamed *her* for Doug's grades.

Olivia's head was spinning. *Flunking?* How can Doug be flunking? And he never told her that his Dad died.

"Now, Miss Rinkle seems to think the world of you. She vouched for you eloquently and sincerely. Against my better judgment, I am going to allow you to remain at Silver Boils. There is one caveat, however . . . that you remain indoors at all times. No more recess. No more field trips. These bears of yours . . . I'll be flummoxed if I have ever heard of such a thing. Did you feed them or something? Why are they so attracted to you?"

"No! I mean . . . I don't know." Olivia stared straight into Mrs. Vitaly's eyes. She could see a little bit of fear in there. A bit of uncertainty.

"We absolutely cannot have this at Silver Boils. Please send them off immediately or I will have to call Wildlife Control. Consider this your last warning, Olivia. You may go."

Olivia wandered slowly down the dark hallway toward Miss Rinkle's classroom. She shouldn't be the one punished. It was Begonia and the Mutches that caused the whole thing. She had lost her father *and* her mother, and no one was walking on eggshells around *her*. No one was worried about *her* flunking or bears hurting *her*. First, they called her a bear charmer, now they were calling her a witch. It was clear that Lyonia was simply not going to accept her. Now, even Doug wouldn't have anything to do with her. She was alone. Only Miss Rinkle cared and she couldn't wait to see her tonight. The class went silent as she entered the room. She plopped down at her desk and stared out the window for the rest of the day.

That evening Miss Rinkle had very little to say as she entered the Milligans' home. From her purse she quietly produced a thick stack of papers and laid them on the kitchen table along with two pencils, a small pencil sharpener, and a thick pink eraser. Aunt, Uncle, and Gnat were out back feeding the pond fish and watering flowers.

"Here. I want you take this test. It is an IQ test," she said, pulling the chair back so Olivia could sit down. "It is *very* important that once you start, you do not stop. It is timed."

Olivia was surprised that Miss Rinkle didn't want to talk about the day's events. She looked at the thick test. "How much time do I have?"

"It isn't how much time you are allowed," Miss Rinkle snipped. "What is important is how much time it takes you to finish it." Olivia didn't like the tone of her voice. She seemed in a hurry.

"Ready . . . set . . . begin!" Miss Rinkle pushed a button on her watch. Olivia turned the first page over.

Carmine is to red, as cerulean is to _____.

Olivia penciled in the word "blue." She remembered that answer from a box of crayons she had when she was younger. Cheeto lay down on her lap, growling quietly in the general direction of Miss Rinkle.

_____ chloride is the composition of table salt.

The questions were hard. She didn't have the foggiest idea what the answer to number two was supposed to be. She thought about finding the Aquaman walkie-talkie and calling Doug. For sure, he knew the answer. But Olivia really wanted to do well on her own. Miss Rinkle seemed so proud of her and what she called her "potential." There were twenty-five questions like that just on page one of the test. After a few minutes, Olivia's head hurt, but she kept going. The rest of the world seemed to disappear as she concentrated on each question.

Hemoglobin is a basic constituent substance in _____.

Olivia wrote "blood" on the line. She began to think maybe she *was* smart enough to answer these questions. Gnat came in, grabbed a Hawaiian Punch from the fridge, and stood next to her smacking his lips. Olivia ignored him.

"Diagnostic commencing," Gnat mumbled and waddled out the back door again. Aunt was out in the yard soaking Uncle with the hose. Olivia didn't even realize that Miss Rinkle had left the room until she heard a crash fifteen minutes later.

"Miss Rinkle?" Olivia called out.

"Go ahead and finish the test, Olivia. I'm all right," she yelled from down the hall.

But Olivia got up anyway and walked toward the sound of the crash. Her bedroom door was cracked open. She pushed it wide. There on the floor, sat Miss Rinkle. She was frantically trying to cram Olivia's clothes back into a dresser drawer that had come tumbling out. The contents of her closet were spread out on the floor.

"You are supposed to finish the test!" Miss Rinkle snapped, her face turning red. "I asked you to finish the IQ test. Now it is all ruined." Realizing the bind she was in, she took a second to calm down. "This has gone on long enough," she said coldly, standing up. "That little episode today is going to ruin everything. We are running out of time." The tone of Miss Rinkle's voice sent chills down Olivia's neck. "It *was* you, wasn't it? A few weeks ago? It was subtle. Very clever. I doubted anyone could even make it work like that. I barely felt it. But you didn't fool me," her eyes darkened. A wave of confusion swept over Olivia. It suddenly occurred to her how much time Miss Rinkle would spend in other rooms during their tutoring sessions. "Where is it?" Miss Rinkle said looking around the room. Her voice was hissing in a sharp whisper. She leaned forward. "Where is it, Olivia? Give it to me."

Just then Uncle walked into the room, smiling and soaked with water. He was wiping his face with a towel. "Hello, ladies, how is class this evening?"

"Oh, Mr. Milligan, your niece is progressing wonderfully!" her sharp nails were digging into the door. She was so phony Olivia wanted to puke. Uncle didn't even seem to notice the awkward situation he walked in on.

"Great. Well, I wanted to let you know that tomorrow it will just be you and Olivia if you don't mind. We have a yoga class in town and Gnat wants to go with us."

"Negative!" Gnat yelled in his loudest voice from down the hall.

Aunt yelled back from the kitchen. "Be a gentleman, Gnat. After yoga we can get some ice cream."

"Negative!"

"And a large pack of batteries for your game," Uncle said, adding to the bribe. Gnat's silence betrayed his agreement to the deal.

Olivia was trying to shake her head *no* so Uncle could see her. She tried to send him a message with ESP.

"Oh, I don't mind at all. I don't have any plans. Take your time. We can make it an extra long class. I'll even make dinner! We don't mind, do we Olivia?" Miss Rinkle turned and pierced Olivia's eyes.

"No! I was kinda thinking of taking tomorrow off. . . ."

"Kind of."

"Huh?"

"Kind of, not kinda." Miss Rinkle had a smirk on her lips.

"Kind of thinking . . ." Olivia continued.

"No, no, Olivia," Uncle butted in. "It is all right. I know how much these classes mean to you. Thank you, Miss Rinkle. You are a blessing." He beamed.

And with that, Miss Rinkle disappeared through the front door.

17

Remembering Junonia

Olivia pretended to have a fever the next morning. And maybe she did have a fever. She hadn't slept at all thinking about what happened with Miss Rinkle.

"I'm siiiiiiiick," she yelled out to the hallway, groaning loudly. Aunt hustled by her room without even looking at her door. Uncle only smiled and said, "Aw you'll be all right with a little rest." She wanted to tell him about what happened. It was on the tip of her tongue, but she held back. He would never believe her. He never believed her about the coral snakes, much less all the crazy stuff that had happened since then. Who would believe her about Miss Rinkle?

It didn't seem to take long for Gnat to leave for school, return in the afternoon, and for the three of them to drive off for yoga class. Olivia slowly opened her door. The house was eerily quiet. She rushed about locking each door. She peeked out the front window. After a few minutes, Miss Rinkle pulled up in her car and knocked. Getting no answer, she knocked louder, then tried the doorknob. The knob rattled and shook as she grew more frustrated. Cheeto was in a complete frenzy, barking at the door. Olivia waited for Miss Rinkle to give up and go home. After several minutes, the rattling stopped. Olivia slowly crept up to the front window again and carefully peeked out from behind the curtain. She was still at the door. Olivia could see her hand on the doorknob. Miss Rinkle closed her eyes. After a few seconds, the knob quietly turned and the door opened.

"Hello, Olivia," Miss Rinkle said, closing the front door behind her. Her long fingers turned the lock tight. "You see, the world is a much bigger, more complex place than you realize." She slipped out of her shoes. To Olivia's astonishment, Miss Rinkle's toes were as long as her fingers. Each toe uncurled from being cramped into her shoes and stretched out. They seemed to grip the floor. She let out a sigh of relief. "I don't know how you people wear these things."

Cheeto prickled underneath Olivia's legs, snarling. Miss Rinkle snapped her hand out and grabbed him by the scruff of his neck. Cheeto squirmed, whining and snarling. But Miss Rinkle didn't lighten her grip. She threw him outside the back door yelping. He turned and lunged back toward the door, but it was too late. He scratched and yowled against the glass. As she turned from the door, the light sparkled red in her hair. Olivia's birthday barrette was clipped neatly in the back.

Miss Rinkle suddenly looked very serious. "I know you've been down to Junonia. I've seen your footprints. I smelled you. I smelled your boyfriend, Doug. I smelled your brother." She stepped slowly closer and closer to Olivia. She was so close their noses almost touched. "Do you want to know what happened down there?"

Olivia slowly nodded her head. She didn't think she had much choice.

"Long ago, Olivia, Florida was not the place that you see today. The oceans were much higher and Florida itself was nothing much beyond a long beach of sandy dunes extending south from Georgia. The land you are standing on right now, the scrub, Lyonia itself, was one of those dunes. Oh, the air was so clear and clean back then! The oceans were filled with the most amazing jellyfish the size of cars. At night, they would glow out there in the sea like enormous pulsing moons," Miss Rinkle said, staring off into the distance. "There were horrible monsters out there too. Sharks the size of houses. Crocodiles bigger than your school bus. Giant, bloodthirsty dire wolves ravaged the dunes hunting for anything they could catch. So the Junonians built their city deep underneath the dunes where they would be safe. Even there, they had to worry about the Crogan horses, but at least those smelly beasts could be domesticated. The Junonians were a strange people. I suppose if you saw them today, you wouldn't even call them people."

Olivia felt herself get caught up in Miss Rinkle's storytelling.

"Life was a brief, violent endeavor for primitive peoples living back then. You see, most people were focused on the *mechanics* of things. Rock smashes coconut. Sharp stick spears fish. That sort of thing. It lends itself to violence and war. But the Junonians weren't into mechanics, they were interested in chemistry and biology. I suppose it came naturally to them. Long before the pyramids of Egypt were built, they *grew* their underground city. Like a bone grows in your leg or a snail secretes its shell. They didn't hack down trees or blast rock out of the ground or enslave other people to do their work. The city just . . . it just emerged. Because the Junonians didn't destroy anything else in order to survive, they lived in harmony with the world around them even as the world around them was filled with anguish. They peaceably farmed vast caverns of fungi and mosses to eat. They learned how to safely walk on the surface to harvest fruits and vegetables. They didn't believe in killing anything, man or animal. And just like those giant jellyfish would light up in the sea, the

Junonians knew how to generate light and energy without electricity. The whole city lights up without the use oil or coal. Just think, Olivia, tens of thousands of years before Thomas Edison, the Junonians were lighting and warming their city."

Olivia remembered how Gnat lit the city with the flashlight. She also remembered Uncle telling her about Edison and Tesla. Miss Rinkle could see that Olivia knew what she was talking about. And Olivia could tell that Miss Rinkle had used Edison's name on purpose. Miss Rinkle continued. "They lived a charmed existence. But they had a secret. Not a bad secret, but an advantage. They called it the Pearl. I think you know what I am talking about now, don't you? Secrets?"

Olivia stared at Miss Rinkle. Something inside her was telling her not to say anything.

"You sure are quiet this evening, Olivia! What happened to my little precocious genius?" Miss Rinkle forced a laugh. "The Pearl gave Junonia much of its power. The Pearl, it is said, controls all of the laws of nature. It protected them and gave them knowledge beyond anything we have today. No one knows where it came from or how the Junonians came to possess it. But in the end, Junonians were still a primitive people. They were frightened of its power. Legends told of their attempts to use the Pearl ending with terrible disasters. The Ice Age itself was caused when the Junonian mayor accidentally tilted the Earth by a half degree. Did you know the Sahara desert used to be a lush jungle? Misusing the Pearl turned it to one big pile of sand. So they stopped trying to use it. Only the highest priest held the knowledge on how to open and safely use the Pearl. His name was Tagelus. No other Junonian was allowed to learn its secrets. They protected it and worshiped it because they knew how important the Pearl was." Miss Rinkle chuckled. "But they had no idea how important it was to *all* of us, to the whole world." Her voice drifted off. "Only Tagelus understood the great responsibility that came with the power of the Pearl. In the wrong hands, even in the hands of a well-meaning person, the Pearl is capable of great destruction. Tagelus possessed the strength of character to resist using its powers. It came to be known as the Pearl of Tagelus. Under the rule of Tagelus, Junonia survived peacefully for a long, long time. When Tagelus died, the secrets of the Pearl died with him."

"Then, thousands of years ago, a Dark Eye like you decided to steal the Pearl."

"D . . . D . . . Dark Eye?" Olivia stammered.

Miss Rinkle smiled warmly. Olivia almost forgot that she wasn't really the friendly teacher she had grown to love. "Remember the people I told you about a few minutes ago that spent all of their time on mechanics, those people that lived on the surface with the dire wolves? Dark Eyes are what we call those among us who do not, or *can*not, see the world as it actually is. They are blinded by greed or arrogance. It is a product of their brutal life. But brutality breeds brutality, Olivia. That one, stupid Dark Eye decided to steal Junonia's only source of protection from its enemies. The resulting war destroyed most of Junonia. The few remaining survivors split up. Some moved to the surface, and there, living among the Dark Eyes, they forgot the old ways. They forgot the peace, they forgot the utter beauty . . . and who knows why? Maybe it was too painful for them to remember. Maybe the sunlight made them greedy. Their eyes grew dark too, and soon even the very thought of the old world, the real world was impossible to them. The Dark Eyes dumped their garbage into sinkholes. They drained their poisons from their mechanical machines. It dripped down through the sands and it befouled Junonia. Those few that chose to stay behind and honor the old ways slowly died out. Junonia became a ghost town. Oh, it is only a pale shadow of what it once was. Dark Eyes just never bother to pay attention." She scowled with more than a hint of disgust.

"Olivia, I am not your enemy. I am your friend and you don't even realize it. I know you will find that hard to believe. I'm sorry that I scared you the other night. It is just you . . . you do not understand. You *can't* understand. I was hoping to frighten you into giving the Pearl to me. But that is good." She nodded. "Very clever of you not to. You were right to not just hand it over lightly. That Pearl is very dangerous, and not just because evil beings want it." Miss Rinkle paused. "How did you get it anyway? How did you get into the chapel? I've never been able . . ."

Olivia shrugged her shoulders.

"Well of course, you are a Guardian. You wouldn't know. Well, it doesn't matter. You can certainly see why I am angry with the Dark Eyes. I watched so much loss, so much pain. They just do not pay attention. They only want to smash things. Oh, you have your stories too. *Myths,* you call them. Your myths have a grain of truth, but only a taste, only a smidgen. The real truth is so much more wonderful. Your horrible little friends call me the Bobwhite Witch. But I am not a witch at all, you see. That is what Dark Eyes do when they see something they don't understand. They react in fear. They are scared of what they don't understand, just like you are a little scared right now. I can feel it." Miss Rinkle smiled.

"But fear is exactly the wrong feeling. Fear is what caused that war in Junonia. Fear is what causes those same kids to call you a bear charmer.

You aren't a bear charmer, are you? You see, you and I are just alike. The *right* thing to do, the way the universe works, is trust. We understand that the way to live is by facing what you don't understand with a full acknowledgment that the universe is the way it is for a reason. Do not be afraid, Olivia. Be open. Open your eyes. There is so much I could teach you. There are so many places I could show you. Junonia is just the beginning. This is an opportunity for you that no other Dark Eye in history can even dream of. With the Pearl, we can restore Junonia to its proper glory. We can end this tyranny of the Dark Eyes. I can even help you find your father and mother. You could be together again." Miss Rinkle's eyes were sparkling blue and wide like Bluejack springs in sunlight. Olivia wanted to swim there.

"Your eyes . . ." she whispered.

"Huh?"

"Your eyes, they used to be gray."

"That's just the lighting. Olivia, show me the Pearl. Let me show you how to work it. How to protect it."

"You called me a Guardian," Olivia whispered. Her voice barely worked. Miss Rinkle had her trapped in the kitchen.

"What?"

"You called me a Guardian," she said louder. "A Guardian. That means it is my job to protect the sphere . . . the . . . the Pearl."

"And I want to help you protect it, Olivia." Miss Rinkle started to sound worried. "You need me to help you."

"I . . . I don't think so," Olivia interrupted. "I think, if you were meant to have it, you would have been able to enter the chapel on your own. I think," Olivia said deliberately, "I think the universe chose me as a Guardian and not you . . . for a reason."

Hearing her own words used against her, Miss Rinkle bristled. "You disrespectful child," she said through clenched teeth. "You don't know what you are talking about." She paused for an uncomfortably long time. Olivia stared at her eyes, never looking away.

Finally, Miss Rinkle began again. "Your mud eaters are getting bold. Too bold. Sick disgusting stupid creatures. You know, they will eat anything, no matter how rotten. Grubs. Stinkhorns. Slugs. Garbage. Rancid carcasses and road kill. It makes them stink. Nasty, greasy beasts. But they cannot help you here Olivia." It took her a second to realize Miss Rinkle was referring to the bears.

"Your aunt and uncle can't help you either. I've been feeding them tarflower berries while they sleep. They believe everything I whisper to them at night. Your aunt has been acting strangely, no? She no longer trusts you, Olivia. She thinks you are a troublemaker. Your uncle . . . your uncle was tougher. He was starting to figure it out. I could tell. No matter how many times I whispered in his ear to throw you out of the house. He was always an optimist. Filled with so much trust for a Dark Eye. So, I did the opposite. I told him that nothing was wrong. I taught him to be happy no matter what. The eternal optimist," she chuckled. "Just in time too. It was only a few nights later that you pulled that little stunt with the gravity. Hmmm . . . I remember him years ago stomping through the woods searching for the Pearl. I watched him. For hours and days he crisscrossed through the paths out there with his little contraptions and maps. He got closer than most. He walked right past the entrance you, Doug, and Gnat fell through."

"Why didn't you just feed me tarflower berries?" Olivia asked.

Miss Rinkle laughed, then almost yelled, "Because, your bedroom floor is covered with coral snakes at night. Strangest thing I've ever seen. Why they would protect a Dark Eye, I'll never know. But I tried everything," she said proudly. "I'm the one that sent you the barrette for your birthday. It brought you to me faster. I was so bored waiting, always waiting."

"This barrette was made hundreds of years ago from a single piece of agatized coral," she said, running her fingers through her hair. "Pretty rare too. Then, just like a typical, fumbling Dark Eye, you went and lost it. When I realized you had been down to Junonia, I decided to pose as your teacher. I had to stay close. Oh, and pretending you were a genius! Oh my, you believed that from the very moment I uttered it, you arrogant child." Miss Rinkle's voice was getting louder and louder. Her eyes squinted tight. "You know, if I felt the gravity disappear the other night, others did as well. It is only a matter of time before they find you, and they won't be so patient and kind. You won't live to see the gopher apple harvest."

"Who? Who will find me?"

"The Cult of Wardenclyffe, for one. Dark Eyes that want the Pearl. Evil creatures you can't even begin to imagine. They won't care about you, Gnat, or your aunt and uncle," she chuckled. "I'm surprised you haven't had a run in with them already." As she spoke, a thick band of red started appearing across her eyes. At first, Olivia thought she was just turning red with anger, or Miss Rinkle had a rash. But it got darker and darker until it was as red as a freshly painted barn. She grabbed Olivia by the shoulders. "I see your uncle has been telling you stories. You are going to end up like him, old and senile. Give it to me now. The Pearl is too powerful for you, Olivia. You are going to get hurt. You are going to destroy the whole world. It will only bring you trouble and death. This is your last chance."

Olivia shook her head slowly. Miss Rinkle gave a screech. "I knew it. I knew it." Her voice barely sounded human. She barely resembled Miss Rinkle anymore. "That first day in the woods. I should have killed you then. I should have ripped your insides out right there. I thought, 'NO! How could this little girl, so dumb that she wore flip-flops into the woods, be the Guardian?' I didn't believe it. Are you even marked? Are you marked? You aren't even marked!" Her voice rose to a painful shrill.

Olivia remembered the strange men at the plantation gas station saying the same thing about a mark. It still didn't make any sense to her. All of these stories were swirling in her head. Miss Rinkle started shaking her by the shoulders. Olivia shoved her hands away and ducked under her flailing arms. The front door swung open and countless bobwhites burst through the opening, rushing toward their queen. Their screeching was almost unbearable and she didn't dare look back. She bolted straight into the living room and clamored over the giant opal boulder. Hunkered down behind the big rock, she loosened a floor board and carefully pulled the Pearl out of the dark crawlspace. She had been coming out here at night and slowly working on the nails in the floor. It was the only place she thought of that was safe. She could hear the Bobwhite Witch scrambling through the house. Her long talons scratched on the wood floor.

"Livi . . . a! Livi . . . a! Where did you go, you little brat?" Only Gnat ever called her Livia. How did the witch know to call her that? But Olivia didn't spend any time thinking about it. Her hands flew over the Pearl. Every night since she'd found it, she had practiced opening it and making it work. Even after she messed up gravity. Even after a drop of molten glass dripped out onto her bed and burned a hole in her sheet. Every mistake, every dead end, every unsolvable switch and panel only strengthened her desire to completely understand it. After all these weeks of practice, it hummed and chimed under her fingers. Even so, she had barely begun to open the Pearl up and solve its mysteries. The Witch heard the Pearl opening and screamed from the other side of the boulder. Olivia sped up. Ruby switch, oak slider, fire button . . . she memorized her path inside. A quartz pyramid twisted and pressed popped open. A flap that, to Olivia, looked made of a butterfly wing opened like a book. She was so absorbed in the Pearl, she barely knew what was going on in the room around her. Finally, the platinum hinge opened under her fingers. A blue bubble of light exploded into the room knocking the witch from her feet. She had discovered the platinum hinge two nights ago and was surprised when Cheeto couldn't get to her through the blue force field.

Olivia stood up. The bubble sparkled and pulsed around her. She was safe inside, but her hands started shaking uncontrollably. As she stepped out from behind the boulder, the sight of Miss Rinkle shocked her. She had become half-bird, half-woman. Her ears were gone. Her arms twisted and her mouth had sharpened into an enormous beaklike structure. All over her skin, little stubs of feathers were peaking through like knitting needles and it seemed like they were growing by the second. Olivia could hardly recognize anything of the Miss Rinkle that pointed a crooked-wood stick at her in class weeks ago. It looked agonizing. Her face contorted. Her arms flailed. The witch flung herself into Olivia's bubble and flew backwards to the floor screaming, followed by a puff of smoke. The bobwhites all strutted and squawked angrily around the room. They pecked at the sofa, yanking the stuffing out. They pulled the books off the shelf. Papers were flying everywhere as if there were a tornado whirling about inside the house. Again and again, the witch launched herself at Olivia only to bounce back.

Olivia pulled the platinum hinge even tighter. The bubble grew larger, pushing the witch and her birds back farther and farther. She started walking toward them. The birds scattered, screeching out the door. Finally giving up, the Bobwhite Witch stopped fighting. She stared at Olivia through the blue bubble for a few seconds. Then, in a flurry of feathers, she turned and swooped angrily out the door. Olivia turned the bubble off and closed the Pearl. Even as she collapsed on the destroyed couch in exhaustion, she knew it wasn't going to be the last time she saw her.

18

Alone

"Hello? Hello? Doug? Are you there?" Olivia was whispering as loudly as she could into the Aquaman walkie-talkie. It had taken her almost an hour to clean up the mess caused by the bobwhites and the witch. She struggled to stuff the cotton back into the sofa cushions, but she was able to put pillows over the obvious tears. She could only hope that Uncle wouldn't try to read one of his books and find that they were out of order. It would be dark before they came home so maybe Aunt wouldn't notice that her beloved philodendron had been tipped over and a leaf had torn, at least for a few days.

"Doug, I need to talk to you." Her voice crackled into the walkie-talkie. She waited several minutes. She really wanted to ask him about how his father died. She wanted to hug him and tell him that she knew how he felt, sort of. The last time she saw him was after the fight with Begonia, Cuke, and the un-twins. He was obviously scared of her now, like it was her fault the bear knocked Begonia down. He hadn't even ridden the bus home with her and Gnat, and she was worried. He was the closest thing she had to a friend in the whole world. Katie had written her a letter a few weeks ago, but it was obvious that she was spending more and more time with Sara. A few months ago Katie didn't even like Sara. Besides, Katie couldn't handle Junonia and this whole mess. But Doug could.

Everything was starting to make sense to Olivia. The bears, the Arabic frogs, the coral snakes, Mr. Gruffle, even the shells and crabs back at the beach. It all had to do with her being the Guardian. Uncle had said that the forces of nature bring the Guardian and the Pearl together by the power of the telluric currents, even if the Guardian is unaware of it happening. That would certainly explain why she ended up here in Lyonia to begin with, why she fell down through the tortoise burrow, and why Junonia's chapel operculum opened for her and not for Gnat or the Bobwhite Witch. She looked underneath her bed. There in the shadows was a hole in the wooden floor where a knot had fallen out of a plank. That must be where the coral snakes enter the house at night. She reached as far as her arm could and ran her finger around the edge of the hole.

Olivia had so many questions with no answers. Did the Pearl of Tagelus sit down there in Junonia for thousands of years untouched? Why didn't another Guardian find it? Most importantly, what was she supposed to do now? Nobody, not even the Bobwhite Witch or Uncle, could tell her what to do now that she had the Pearl.

She *had* to talk to Doug.

"Hello? Pick up! Doug. *Hello!*" Only static crinkled and popped through the speaker. Olivia walked to the kitchen and tried calling him on the telephone. The Corcorans' answering machine picked up and she slammed the phone back into the cradle. He must really be scared. Or his mother wasn't going to allow him to talk to her anymore. Well, she will show *her*. She'll just corner him at school lunch tomorrow.

Aunt and Uncle came home with barely a stir. Gnat marched by with dried ice cream smeared all around his mouth. "We had yoga and ice cream," he announced.

The night was quiet. The frogs had decided to take the night off from their usual croakings and chants. Olivia even cracked her bedroom window to listen for any crickets out there. Nothing. She had gotten so used to the noisy racket outside, now that it was gone, the silence was overwhelming. The silence throbbed in her ears. Olivia looked out the window to the moonlit scrub. A bear sprawled out, asleep in the crook of the old lightning pine. His legs hung down loosely from the branches.

She could only hear the faint sound of Gnat's video game coming from the bedroom next door. "Gnat is too young and stupid to be caught up in this," she thought. It seemed like only a short time ago that Mom was home from overseas and he was born. It was the only time she could remember Mom being at home. And she had stayed for a whole year. She remembered Mom and Dad crying a lot, but she thought the little baby was kind of funny. Certainly nothing to cry about. Even back then, Gnat was a loudmouth. He used to blab away all through the night. Then, when everyone else was tired, he would sleep all day.

Her favorite memory though was one day after church when she and Mom drove two counties to Rabbit Rock, just the two of them. They scrambled up the steep sandstone all the way to the top and ate sandwiches. They were so high up, she could see the *topside* of the hawks flying below. Clouds tumbled and slipped over the vast, golden prairie as the wind blew unimpeded through their hair. Mom told her that she had learned the secret path to the top when she was a young girl herself. Almost no one knew how to get up there. Just a few old-timers and they weren't telling anyone because they thought it was too dangerous. Olivia could hear other people climbing down below, frustrated with the steep crumbly rock. One by one, they each gave up and returned to the picnic tables by the small parking lot. They were completely alone, and she rested her head on Mom's blue dress and the sunny afternoon lingered forever.

Who would have imagined that just five years later, she would be responsible for the most important object in the history of the world and fighting for her life? She wished she could ask Mom what to do. Certainly *she* knew how to fight and do the right thing.

To make matters worse, now when she called Dad, the phone company said that the number was out of service. It didn't even allow her to leave a message.

19

Alphonse

Gnat and Olivia sat by themselves in the very back seat of the blue bus. All of the other children filled the front seats until they were overflowing. Even Larry let little Julie sit on his lap so she could stay close to the driver. If Mr. Ott would allow them to sit on the hood, Olivia was sure a bunch of them would oblige. But she wasn't worried about it. She was wondering why Doug wasn't there. His mother must have driven him to school so he wouldn't have to ride the bus with her.

It wasn't until Olivia was walking down the hallway of Silver Boils Elementary that it occurred to her that Miss Rinkle would be waiting for her behind the classroom door. A wave of dread swept over her. She didn't have the Pearl with her so she wouldn't be able to rely on the blue force field. But surely Miss Rinkle wouldn't do anything with a whole classroom of children watching her.

After a few moments, Mrs. Vitaly came striding down the hallway holding a large pile of papers. With her free hand, she grabbed Olivia's elbow and hustled her into the class.

"Come along, Olivia. We have much to discuss." Mrs. Vitaly's voice was very serious.

As she entered the room, Olivia noticed that Miss Rinkle was *not* sitting at her desk. She looked around. Doug was absent.

"Ummm," she said, "where is Miss . . ."

"Have a seat Olivia," Mrs. Vitaly interrupted, clapping her hands. "Children! Children! Let's pay attention!"

Mrs. Vitaly waited for the whispers and murmurs to quiet down before beginning again.

"I have some potentially disruptive information for you," she announced loudly. "Miss Rinkle will no longer be teaching at Silver Boils. For the remainder of summer session, I will be your instructor."

The class erupted.

Mrs. Vitaly raised her voice above the chaos. "Furthermore, Miss Rinkle left behind neither lesson plans nor your marks. None of the requisite paperwork has even been started. Frankly, I do not know what she has been doing all summer."

The class became hysterical. Cuke immediately seized the opportunity and piped up. "I've been studyin' hard and gettin' A's."

"Yeah, me too," said Larry. Richard punched him. "I mean, us too."

Cuke shot him a mean look and shoved Larry's books onto the floor. "She ain't gonna believe us if we *all* say it," he whispered loud enough for Mrs. Vitaly to hear.

"Class! Please. Let's remain seated."

A fourth grader raised her hand and squirmed in her seat. "Yes, Amelia. You have a question?"

"What happened to Miss Rinkle?" she squeaked.

"At this time, the Catkin County Board of Education has instructed me to neither divulge nor insinuate as to the whereabouts of Miss Rinkle. There are significant legal implications. . . ." Mrs. Vitaly noticed the confused and blank look on Amelia's face. "Uhhhhh . . . I don't know where

Miss Rinkle is," Mrs. Vitaly said definitively. That answer seemed satisfactory to Amelia.

"Normally, I would begin the process of reevaluating your progress and producing the necessary documentation. However, classes are being temporarily suspended due to the formation of a large hurricane off the coast. We apologize for the late decision, but as of last night, there was no record of the hurricane by the National Weather Service. I have reviewed our registration forms and they are indeed up to date, so either the Weather Service failed to comply with the standards of notification, or the hurricane formed quickly overnight." She paused, clearly pleased that she would not be held accountable for the late notice. She continued, this time reading from a sheet of paper.

" 'Hurricane Alphonse is classified as a category four storm and is considered very dangerous. The storm is showing signs of intensifying. You will be bussed back to your homes. However, a signature of receipt is required by your parents and/or legal guardian. If no signature is collected, you will be returned to Silver Boils until pick-up arrangements can be made. Silver Boils serves as a class-2 emergency shelter so your safety is assured. A voluntary evacuation order is in place for Catkin County as the storm is expected to start impacting the area this evening. For those of you with family living near the coast, please inform them that they may be under a mandatory evacuation order. Upon successful conclusion of the storm, classes will resume as scheduled. All emergency shelter questions should be directed to the Lyonia Fire Department. All scholastic questions should be addressed to Mrs. Desiree Vitaly,' " she said, setting the paper down. Someone in the back of the classroom snickered. Her eyes peered out over her reading glasses. "Any questions?"

Olivia raised her hand.

"Yes, Olivia."

The entire class turned to face her.

"I was wondering where Doug is. Does he know about the hurricane?"

"Mrs. Corcoran called me this morning with the news that Doug is ill. I informed her of the hurricane at that time."

"All right, children. Go ahead and gather your personal belongings in an orderly fashion. We will be boarding the buses in ten minutes. I will be taking role call as you board."

A hurricane! Olivia had never been in a hurricane before. She wondered if it was like a tornado. She had sat lots of times with Gnat and Dad in the basement while the Sun Prairie tornado sirens wailed during bad storms. They even interrupted school so the kids could huddle in the hallways. Once, a tornado destroyed a house just a few blocks away. But never a hurricane. She wondered what it was going to be like. As Mrs. Vitaly checked off her name at the bus, Olivia noticed a couple of men wearing sunglasses and standing by a brand-new tan car. They seemed to be monitoring the progress of the evacuation as they talked on their cell phones. One of them was writing on a pad of paper.

Olivia grabbed Gnat's hand and boarded the bus. "Paws off," he said and tried to pull his hand away. "Storm warriors don't hold hands."

"Don't fight, Gnat. Just come on." Olivia gripped his hand tighter.

Just thirty minutes ago, none of the kids would sit within half-a-bus of Olivia. Now, they didn't seem concerned where she sat at all. They were all chattering wildly about the hurricane and Miss Rinkle. Julie even smiled at her. Olivia looked out the window. It sure didn't look like a storm was coming. The sun was blazing as hard as ever.

As the bus pulled out, the tan car turned to follow. The kids were exploding with energy. Most of them couldn't even sit down. The bus stopped at a stop sign. Mr. Ott's eyes jumped back and forth between the mirror and the intersection. He squinted for a moment, then pushed the accelerator all the way to the floor. Gravel flew from beneath the tires. All of the children fell back into their seats. The bus veered around a utility truck and rushed down the highway. Thick oily clouds of smoke billowed from the exhaust.

Cucumber Nevels and the Mutch twins got off at their stop. Their parents signed Mr. Ott's clipboard and hurried their kids down the driveway. So far everything was going to plan. All of the parents had been waiting for their children at the bus stops. A feeling of urgent efficiency permeated the air. The route was almost over.

Mr. Ott eyed Olivia and Gnat in his oversized rearview mirror.

"One of your guardians better be waiting for us. I am not going to drive you all the way back to school," he growled. "You two think I'm going to waste my time driving all over the county with a hurricane bearing down on us, you got another thing coming. You two have been nothing but trouble."

Olivia stared back at him without saying a word. Something about Mr. Ott's bright red face in the mirror made her smile. Gnat wasn't sure if he was getting grounded or not, so he never looked up from his game.

As the rusty blue bus rounded the curve in the highway, Mr. Ott cleared his throat. He could see police lights flashing up ahead at the stop. He gripped the steering wheel tighter. "See? I told you so. Trouble."

The bus rattled to a stop. Seeing the police car, the tan car that had been following them sped around the bus and disappeared down the highway.

"Hey! The stop sign is up!" Mr. Ott yelled.

A police officer walked up to the bus.

"Officer, that car just broke the regulations. It passed illegally."

"Yessir. Are Olivia and Nathan Brophie on board?"

"Uh . . . yes. But I would like that car arrested." Olivia and Gnat tumbled out of the bus.

The officer started walking the two children toward the house.

'Hey! I need signatures," Mr. Ott said, holding out a clipboard. "Here . . . and here."

The officer signed his name. Mr. Ott wasted no time shutting the doors and pulling away. He was almost smiling as he accelerated down the road.

"Don't be alarmed," the officer said, putting his arms around the children. "There has been a break-in, and nobody is hurt. My name is Officer Hugh."

"A break-in?" Olivia repeated.

"Yes, Olivia. We have not identified any missing assets. The house has been practically dismantled though."

"Did they, the burg . . u . . lars, steal my Space Laser?" Gnat was panicking.

"We don't believe so, but one of the things we want you to do is check all of your things."

Aunt came running out of the house followed closely by Cheeto. She lifted Gnat up and kissed his forehead.

"Everyone is fine. Everyone is fine," she said. "We were getting gas and groceries in town and came back to this . . . this mess!"

She was right. Every single decoration, every single book, every cushion, every curtain, every mattress, every drawer lay tossed onto the floor. Pillows were ripped open. The television was smashed. Cheeto ran around the house smelling everything and growling. Olivia looked behind the opal boulder. All of the floor boards were pulled up. It confirmed what she suspected. It was the Bobwhite Witch. Gnat walked out of his room engrossed in a game of space laser.

"Officer Hugh? Do you know who did it?" she asked.

"Errr . . . I'm afraid not. If they didn't actually steal anything, it is unlikely we will ever find the culprits."

"Oh."

"This really is quite unusual here. Usually when they break in, they at least take the TV," Officer Hugh said, frowning at the forty-year-old, black-and-white television on the floor. "They were probably looking for something specific. Did y'all have something valuable that people knew about?"

Aunt and Uncle looked at each other and shook their heads. "We don't think so," they said in unison.

Uncle slapped the opal boulder. "Just this baby," he said proudly. Aunt rolled her eyes.

"Well, I don't think anyone is walking away with that . . . that thing, sir," Officer Hugh said. "How did you get that in here anyway? It's bigger than the doorway."

"He tore down that wall," Aunt said, pointing to the living room wall. The faint, jagged outline could be seen where Uncle had torn open the wall years ago.

"Well, I have everything I need for the report. If you find anything missing, please call this number." He handed Uncle a business card. "I'm sure we will be difficult to contact during Alphonse, but I promise to be in touch when things settle down."

"Thank you, Hugh. We know you will do everything you can. Say hello to your mother for me," Aunt said, closing the door behind her. "I don't know what it is," she said, "but I feel better than I have for weeks. Isn't that weird? Even with the house looking like this. Come on, kids. Let's eat some lunch and then we will clean up this disaster. We should start seeing the hurricane soon. Olivia, you look exhausted."

As the first buttered slices of bread hit the frying pan and started sizzling, Uncle peaked around the corner.

"Pssssssst! Olivia," he whispered.

Olivia turned her head and looked at him.

"Pssssst, come here."

"You don't have to psssst at me," she announced loudly. Suddenly exposed, Uncle fumbled backwards into the living room, crashing into a table. Aunt never even looked up from the grilled cheese sandwiches.

"Look, the Teslatron is still here," he said, relieved when Olivia walked into the living room. "I didn't want to tell Hugh about it, but all I kept thinking was that Wardenclyffe spies must have been here." He carefully placed the Teslatron back into its custom-built protective box.

Olivia knew she had to tell him what had been happening. She didn't know what else to do. Things were only going to get worse if she didn't get some help. Things were getting serious. Next time, the witch might just burn the house down or hurt somebody. She took a deep breath, "I have to tell you something. I'm the Guardi . . ."

"Lunch is ready!" Aunt boomed from the kitchen. "Get out here *now!*"

Uncle stood up and started walking toward the food. "What was that, Olivia?"

"I'm . . . I'm the Guardian." She spit it out.

"How could you possibly . . . That isn't . . . How do you know *that?*" he stuttered. "Don't be silly. That was only a story. Come on, let's eat."

"But I have the sphere. Except it isn't the sphere, it's called the Pearl of Tagelus. I *am* the Guardian. And *you* know it isn't just a story or you wouldn't be so worried about Wardenclyffe spies."

Uncle's face went white. But they were in the kitchen now and Aunt was standing with her hands on her hips.

"Uh . . . Olivia and I are going to take our lunch into the living room and start loading the books back up," he whimpered.

"Nonsense, Harold. Sit down and eat your lunch before it gets cold," Aunt snipped. "Here you go, Olivia. What did they tell you at school this morning?"

"Miss Rinkle is gone. She isn't teaching anymore and they won't say what happened."

"Gone? Why? But how are you going to have your lessons?"

"I don't think she wants to do lessons anymore," Olivia said.

"Why on earth not? I could tell she really enjoyed . . . I hope she is all right." Aunt ran to the telephone to call her gossip contacts in town.

With Aunt out of the room, Uncle grabbed Olivia's arm. She smacked her lips as the melted cheese and sweet tea hit her tongue. "What is going on?" he demanded.

"Miss Rinkle was really the Witch, the Bobwhite Witch."

Uncle looked relieved. "A witch? There are no such things as witches, Olivia. At least not in the storybook sense. I can understand your overactive imagination. It must be overwhelmed with the move here and missing your parents."

"You are the one who taught me to always say yes to the possibilities," she protested.

"Come on, Olivia, let's stop the wild stories for now. Let's be quiet for a while."

But Olivia felt good getting it off her chest. The pressure of keeping it all secret had worn her out. There was no stopping it now. "We found it in Junonia. The Pearl, I mean. Miss Rinkle wanted it. That is why she was our teacher, but she was only pretending to be our teacher. She must be the one that tore up our house today. She didn't get it though. I hid it somewhere else." Boy, that grilled cheese was delicious. Olivia licked her fingers.

"Junonia?"

"Under the sand, the caves out by the springs," she replied. "The old city."

"Yeah. Where Squirt lives," Gnat interjected, grabbing a handful of potato chips.

"Squirt?" Uncle's eyes were filled with incredulity as he slowly turned toward Gnat. Maybe things were starting to connect with Uncle. "But there aren't any caves down . . ."

"And it isn't an encyclopedia like you said. It actually *controls* the laws of nature."

Uncle's jaw was on the ground. "It controls the laws? Of course. Of course! It controls the laws! That explains the third pole. The . . . the . . .

the Pearl must pull the telluric currents to it," he said triumphantly. "The quartz sand out here probably disrupts the coherence of the signal. Now the Pearl has surfaced. That is why the Teslatron has been acting strange lately. You must show it to me," he demanded.

"Nope," she answered.

"What do you mean, 'nope'?" he said.

"I mean NOPE," she replied.

"You . . . must. I mean, you should . . . I've been searching for it my whole life, and my father before me," he whined. "You show up in Florida and find it without even trying. Even Gnat knows about it."

"I can't do that, it is hidden. If I go get it now, Miss Rinkle will see me," she said. "Besides, I'm the Guardian. I'm the only one that should have it. Even you said that."

"I did?"

"Yup," she answered.

"Well, if that is the case, listen very carefully. The Pearl is very powerful, Olivia. You shouldn't be goofing around with it. You have a very grave responsibility."

"Maybe I don't *want* it," Olivia pouted. "You sound just like the witch."

"You see," Uncle said sternly, "you aren't given this kind of responsibility, this kind of destiny, because you *want* it. Millions of people *want* it. Greatness isn't bestowed upon you like a crown or family crest. You, Olivia, have been chosen by the Universe to protect the Pearl because of who you are, in here," he said, pushing his finger at her heart.

Even though Uncle sounded like he was scolding her, his words gave her comfort.

"The bears that have been hanging around, Thunder, the coral snakes, all that . . ." He was clearly piecing it together. Aunt came back into the room and hung up the phone. Just as she did, she thought of someone else to call and picked it up again.

"My goodness, you aren't safe," Uncle said. "*We* aren't safe. If they know you have it . . . Wait. Who, *exactly*, is Squirt?"

"An echinoid," Gnat said.

"A cave urchin," Olivia added. "There are tons of 'em. And there weren't any sprites like you said."

"And Junonia is . . . an underground city?"

"Yes. Well, it's the whole place. I think. But no one really lives there anymore."

"'Cept for the bridge," Gnat added, finishing his last bite and looking up from his empty plate.

"The bridge . . . huh?" Uncle was confused.

"Uncle?" Olivia whispered as quietly as possible.

"What is it?" Uncle answered.

"How old . . . are . . . you?" she asked.

His eyes sharpened to a fine pinprick of light. A slight smile came across his lips. "It's the third pole, Olivia. Don't you feel it?"

"Well, no one seems to be able to account for Miss Rinkle," Aunt suddenly interrupted, hanging the phone up for good. "We might as well clean this disaster up."

For the rest of the afternoon, they cleaned up the house. Olivia was in charge of books. Gnat had his bedroom. Aunt fixed up the kitchen. Uncle worked on re-attaching the floorboards and moving the furniture back to their proper spots. He kept sneaking by and asking questions about

Junonia and the Pearl. As they picked up the mess, Alphonse was picking up outside. She could hear the wind flowing like an invisible torrent. Sometimes, the wind caught the edges of the old house and Olivia could almost feel the structure resist its pull.

The phone rang.

"NO!" Aunt screamed from the other room. She rushed into the kitchen, holding the phone against her chest. "It's Mrs. Corcoran. Doug! He's missing. She was calling to see if we've seen him. Do you know where he is, Olivia?"

"He wasn't at school, and I tried calling him last night," she replied. But she knew Doug was too much of a chicken to just run away.

Aunt put the phone back up to her ear. "I'm sorry Eloise . . . no . . . no she doesn't. I will. Of course. Let us know if there is anything we can do. Goodbye."

"The whole county is out looking for him again," Aunt said. "Lord, I hope they find him before the hurricane hits. What else can go wrong today?"

Olivia took Cheeto outside as the last of the evening light hung in the air. The sky was sliding overhead like a giant gray sheet. The trees were twisting and swaying like crazy jazz dancers in the warm wind. Bits of flower petal, floating seeds, oak leaves, and tiny moths flew out of control in a great whirl, caught up in winds larger than themselves. She looked up into the spinning world. The entire planet was moving and shifting. Every detail shook and flailed. A moment of fear flashed through her heart. What if everything in the world was apt to be wiped away, like the dirt she had swept up from Aunt's broken houseplants? It was the kind of thing she would have to start considering now. Gently, she felt a wet nose push into her hand. Olivia looked down to see a very small bear standing next to her.

"There, there," she said, rubbing its ear. "Everything will be all right."

20

Hoolie

The air conditioner rattled and sputtered until, after thirty years of faithful service, it stopped. Olivia awoke with a jump at the sudden silence. Almost as quickly, she could feel the outdoor air sneak into the room and gather into warm drafts. The full brunt of Alphonse was not supposed to land until sunrise, so the Milligans had decided to get some sleep before the worst of it hit. They hadn't predicted the untimely demise of their air conditioner.

Within a few minutes, she could hear Uncle out back, slamming a disturbingly long wrench onto the broadside of the condenser unit. Olivia peeked over the edge of her bed. To her relief, she didn't see any snakes on the floor. The wind suddenly roared. The tropical rains started again, pelting onto the sides of the house. For some reason, Olivia had expected a lot of lightning and thunder during the hurricane. She was surprised that, in fact, there wasn't any all.

She was awake. Wide awake.

What to do? She stared at the ceiling. She followed the ceiling fan to see if she could watch a single blade spinning around — she couldn't. She counted the number of times Uncle hit the air conditioner — 43. Then he gave up. Maybe the frogs left her another message. Olivia grabbed the curtain and flung it aside. What she saw caused her mouth to go dry.

Scratched directly into the glass was the message:

Doug for Pearl. Tonight.

The Witch! She had kidnapped Doug in order to get the Pearl. Her skin crawled to think of what she would do to him with her poisons. She looked out into the storm. The tree branches were breaking off at all angles. She wondered if her bears were safe out there. She looked down to the ground. There, shining on the sand under the window, were the white bellies of three dead frogs. A single cactus spine pierced the heart of each one.

Olivia rushed to get dressed. She didn't know what she was going to do, but she knew she had to do something. The one thing she didn't have to figure out was where the Bobwhite Witch was hiding Doug. They were in Junonia. Waiting for her. She was sure of it. She put her shoes on so quickly she forgot Aunt's advice to look inside first. Even though it seemed too warm for a jacket, she slipped on a windbreaker. Her hands shook as she zipped up. She heard Alphonse pouring against the house so aggressively she feared it would come rushing inside with an explosion of leaves and small branches and glass.

Then she heard a quiet tapping. TAP. TAP. She looked around. Where was it coming from? TAP. TAP. TAP. Then, in a brief moment of calm wind, she heard it.

"SQUEAK!"

Squirt was outside on the window sill, tapping his stony body against the glass. Olivia ran to the window and opened it. The wind rushed into the room and swung the curtains up over her head. Squirt jumped from the sill onto her hand.

"Squirt! You came to find me!"

"SQUEAK. SQUEAK." Squirt was shaking and agitated. A reddish color flushed over his body. Olivia raised him up close to her face. She kissed him on his star.

"It's all right, cutie. You made it here. You must have really had an adventure walking . . . er . . . sliding here through the woods. You like the rain huh?"

"SQUEAK. SQUEAK. SQUEAK."

"I hate to do this to you, but we have to go get Doug. All the way back in Junonia. This time, you can ride in here," she said, slipping him into her pocket. She packed the Aquaman walkie-talkie, a flashlight, and extra batteries into her backpack. She noticed a peanut in the bottom which she removed and dropped into her pocket. Squirt immediately pounced on the treat. His violent squirming and munching tickled Olivia's leg.

"I'll get some more treats from the kitchen," she said, opening the bedroom door. As she walked down the hallway, she heard talking in the living room. She didn't recognize the voices.

"Where is it, Harold? We would hate to go wake the kids now, wouldn't we?" The stranger's voice sounded raspy and very tired. "We know you have it."

Olivia stepped carefully on the creaky floor boards.

"I really have to give you credit," the voice said. "After all these years, we started to think you were a crackpot with your . . . what do you call it? . . . your Teslatron?" The man laughed. But it wasn't a fun laugh. It creeped Olivia out.

Carefully, she peeked around the corner. Both Aunt and Uncle were sitting on wooden chairs. Their hands were tied behind their backs. Aunt's mouth was gagged so she couldn't scream. Olivia could see that she had been crying. Two men were standing behind them. They were the same men that had followed her bus home from school yesterday. One of them leaned down and whispered in Uncle's ear.

"All right. Fine. I *am* the Guardian," Uncle said. Crying, Aunt turned to look at him and shook her head. "I found the sphere down by the old fernery," he continued. "But I'm *not* going to give it to you if you hurt my family."

Olivia saw the man grab Uncle's neck. It looked like it hurt. She couldn't believe that Uncle was telling the strangers that *he* was the Guardian.

"I *am* going to hurt your family. I promise you. I am going to hurt them right now," the stranger sneered. "I will find where you hid it on my own. I'm beginning to think that I don't need any of you anymore." The second man pulled a knife out of his pocket and flashed it in front of Aunt and Uncle.

Olivia ran as quickly and quietly as she could to Gnat's room. He was snoring loudly with all of the sheets and covers on the floor.

"Gnat! Gnat! Wake up!" she whispered and shook him. "Gnat!"

"Huh? Wha?" he mumbled, sitting up.

"Get dressed, now. And don't make a single noise," she ordered.

"Is it the hurricane?" he asked.

"No. It's the Cult of Wardenclyffe. We have to get out of here. Be quiet!" Gnat seemed more confused than ever, but he obeyed.

They walked quietly to the back door.

"Wait here a sec," Olivia whispered as she snuck toward the living room. Suddenly she stopped. The strangers were pushing Aunt and Uncle toward the front door. They were going to see her if she didn't move quickly. Olivia whipped around. Her arm hit a small Japanese gong sitting on a table. It clattered to the floor and rang through the house.

"Gnat! Run!" Olivia yelled, scrambling toward the back.

She looked back over her shoulder. One of the men dragged Aunt and Uncle toward the front door. The man was screaming, "They've seen us! They've seen us!" The man with the knife lunged across the room toward her. Uncle threw his body into the man with the knife and ran toward Olivia.

"Sky Island, Olivia! Sky Island!" he yelled, but the other stranger grabbed him by the arm and slammed him into the wall. Uncle was knocked out cold. More men jumped through the door.

Olivia stumbled through the back door, picking Gnat up along the way. A blast of wind almost pushed her over, but she shoved her way through it. They sprinted toward the woods. Rain pelted their faces. Cheeto scrambled into the woods. Gnat was crying.

Out of the darkness, several more men stepped in front of them. Olivia recognized one of the men from the gas station. His greasy hair glistened in the night.

"Where do you think you are going?" he said, laughing. Olivia could see his sharp, yellow teeth. "You remember me, Little Thing?" He stroked her cheek with the back of his hand. "I remember you. Little Thing is lucky that her Uncle is the Guardian. But it seems her luck has run out." The other men came through the back door. Olivia and Gnat were surrounded.

"Turn right around and go back inside," the greasy-haired man ordered.

"You let my Uncle and Aunt go!" Olivia yelled. "I know who you are!"

The men looked at each other and laughed. Suddenly, one of the men screamed out and grabbed for his face. He twisted in agony into the light and Olivia saw what was tormenting him. A walkingstick was firmly attached to his face and squirting him with noxious poisons. From the tops of the trees, the other walkingsticks launched themselves into the wind, soaring down at the men like kamikaze pilots. Maybe they had not forgotten the kindness of Olivia and her uncle. The men flailed their arms at the unseen attackers.

Olivia and Gnat darted between the men and ran for the woods. As they reached the first trees, Olivia turned and saw several men chasing them. Their flashlights pierced through the darkness. She couldn't believe how overwhelming the storm was as it raged through the woods. Branches fell all around. Faster and faster they ran. One stranger snagged his shirt on an oak branch, giving them a chance to get farther ahead.

Then, standing on the sand up ahead, a bear! And a big one! Without hesitating, Olivia picked up Gnat again and launched herself into the air. They landed smack on the bear's back. As they grabbed onto his think fur, she noticed a cinnamon tuft of hair on his head.

"Thunder?" she yelled out. No. This bear was too young. It must be Thunder's son. Olivia suddenly felt a whole lot safer.

"Go!" she ordered. "Go, Hoolie!" The bear turned and bolted into the woods.

Gnat turned his head and looked at Olivia. "Hoolie?" he asked, still crying.

"Just hang on!" Olivia scolded. She didn't have time to explain how names just came to her.

Bullets zinged through the air above them. They turned onto a secret bear highway and within seconds, the Wardenclyffe thugs were left far behind. Another bear joined them, running alongside Hoolie. Soon another and another. Before long, over ten bears were crashing through the forest with Olivia and Gnat. Their heavy footsteps rumbled. A tree fell to the ground behind them, blown over by the storm. Leaves and debris flew everywhere. The rain stung their eyes.

They could hear ATVs racing after them. A couple of bears turned back from the group to confront the strangers. Olivia heard gunshots and screaming.

"Stop!" Olivia screamed, pulling on Hoolie's fur as they reached an opening in the forest. The big bear skidded to a stop. The other bears looked nervous and paced in circles around the clearing. Olivia jumped off Hoolie's back and walked over to the edge of the clearing. She knelt down on all fours.

"Hurry," Gnat whined.

"Mr. Gruffle. Mr. Gruffle. Are you home?" she called down into the old tortoise's burrow. Hoolie tilted his head, confused by Olivia's behavior.

After a few moments, the venerable tortoise poked his head out of the darkness.

"I need the Pearl, Mr. Gruffle," Olivia asked. "Please?" He disappeared down into his burrow. A minute later, a time interval that seemed like an eternity to Olivia but was actually quite brisk for a tortoise, he rolled the shining blue Pearl up the sloping burrow like a miniature bulldozer. The surrounding trees lit up with its blue glow. She had known after her confrontation with the Bobwhite Witch that she would come back to the house. That day, after cleaning up the mess from their fight, she had snuck out here to hide the Pearl in the only safe place she could think of.

"Thank you. You are the sweetest." Olivia rubbed the leathery skin of his throat with her index finger. Mr. Gruffle stretched his neck to its full length and pushed into her finger. It is rare for a tortoise to be rubbed on the throat and they love it so.

Olivia tucked the Pearl into the backpack. The two bears that had gone back to fight the ATVs stumbled back into the clearing. One was limping, but it didn't bother him enough to stop him. Olivia climbed onto Hoolie's back and the bears started running again.

"Goodbye, Mr. Gruffle," Olivia yelled back as they disappeared into the stormy brush.

They ran through the site of the Acorn War. They ran past Bluejack Springs. Those days of wandering through the scrub planting flags on tortoise burrows seemed like a lifetime ago. The sound of more ATVs carried on the wind. Olivia and Gnat were soaked. The rain fell so fast, Olivia couldn't see beyond Hoolie's nose. It seemed like the branches and falling trees were *trying* to hit them as they ran toward the entrance of Junonia. Hoolie struggled to make any forward progress in the buffeting wind. The bears slowed to a mere crawl. The ATVs rushed closer and closer. Olivia could see their spotlights swinging through the dark woods behind them.

"There!" she leaned forward and yelled into Hoolie's ear so he could hear her over the wind. She pointed toward the sandy clearing with the old burrow in the center. "You have to run into it just right! You can't be afraid or it won't work!"

One after another, the bears leapt into the burrow and disappeared.

Finally, Hoolie plunged with all of his might into the wet sand. Down they tumbled. Both Gnat and Olivia lost their grip on his back. They held their breath until they fell out of the sand and into the midair. One big pile of bear, child, and backpack crashed onto the mountain of white sand at the end of the tombolo.

They were back in Junonia.

21

The Battle

Each bear stood up and shook the sand out of his fur. Hoolie had landed on Olivia's legs, so she had to wait for him to stand up. They were back in the cave. This time, Olivia wasn't so much afraid of the enormous and dark cavern. She was more concerned about the witch. Olivia's mind raced on how she could safely retrieve Doug and not lose the Pearl too. She couldn't come up with any ideas.

The cave roared and shook with the falling hurricane rains. The waterfalls were so violent it reminded Olivia of the trip she, Dad, and Gnat had taken to Copper Falls two summers ago. Gnat was too young to remember when they stood on the rocks to let the pounding river crash and spray all over them.

Because it was the middle of night, the cave was dark. Very dark. Olivia fumbled around in her backpack, searching for her flashlight. She felt her pocket heat up. Squirt jumped furiously. She reached in and pulled him out. He glowed brighter than she had ever seen, like a charcoal briquette in a grill. He was so bright she couldn't look directly at him. Out in the water, she could see other cave urchins starting to glow like stars in the night. It gave the bears just enough light to find their way.

"I'm not walking this time," Gnat said, scrambling onto Hoolie's back. Hoolie rolled his eyes. Olivia walked up to him.

"Thank you for saving us," she said, kissing him on the mouth. The bear seemed so happy his skin quivered.

"You *are* Thunder's son, aren't you?" she asked with one hand on his cheek.

At the mention of his father's name, Hoolie stomped both paws into the sand.   Once everyone had adjusted to the cave, Olivia climbed back up on Hoolie's back and pointed toward the tombolo.

"Let's go," she said.

Hoolie didn't move.

"Let's run! Go!" Olivia yelled louder. None of the bears twitched a muscle.

"OK. Have it your way. Gnat, come on," she said, getting down. She was pretty sure kicking Hoolie like he was a horse would be a bad idea.

"I'm not walking this time," Gnat repeated.

"Yes," she ordered, "you are." She pulled his arm hard enough to dismount him. Lit by hundreds of glowing cave urchins, she stormed off down the tombolo dragging Gnat behind her.

As Olivia and Gnat disappeared into the darkness, Hoolie let out a long, heavy sigh. Within seconds, the kids were sitting on his back and the bears were jogging through the cave.

"I told you I wasn't walking this time," Gnat said.

The long tombolo went by much faster as the bears picked up their pace. Everyone was soaked and covered with a thin layer of sand. Suddenly the bears all stopped. One by one, they pushed off the sand with their front paws and stood on their hind legs. Hoolie grunted loudly and stood up too. Olivia and Gnat hung on to his back with all their might. It felt like they were ten feet off the ground. The bears were huffing and gnarling and snapping their jaws. Olivia looked around Hoolie's head and she instantly saw why they had stopped.

Standing in the path in front of them was one of the mammoth skeletons. To Olivia's shock, the skeleton stomped its enormous bony foot and swung its trunk from side to side. A dusty bellow trumpeted out of the end of its trunk. The bright armor draped over its bones glinted and sparkled. Its tusks seemed sharper and longer than ever. Out of the darkness another one appeared. And another. Time had not been kind to some of them. One was missing a tusk. Another's armor was falling apart as it moved. One had only two legs and it struggled helplessly to right itself. Its moaning filled the cave.

Then, behind the bears, another armored mammoth skeleton rose up out of the sand. They were surrounded! Their hollow eye sockets stared dumbly. It wasn't that long ago they had found shelter inside the ribcage of one of these mammoths. The bears circled around Hoolie and the kids.

From behind the line of mammoth skeletons, another one approached. The mammoths lumbered to the side to make room for the new one. This mammoth was bigger and more elaborately armored than the others. High atop, straddling the enormous vertebrae of its neck, sat Miss Rinkle. Sitting in front of her, droopy-eyed and exhausted, was Doug.

"Ahhhhhh, Miss Olivia. How nice of you to join us!" Miss Rinkle yelled out. "How do you like my little hurricane? It wasn't easy to concoct that one so quickly."

"I think your hurricane is wimpy," Olivia yelled back.

Miss Rinkle seemed perturbed at the taunt. "You are surrounded. You better just give me the Pearl. You can all leave in peace if you give it to me."

"Give me Doug first," she responded, gripping the straps of her backpack harder.

"*You* are not making the demands here. I know Wardenclyffe has your Aunt and Uncle. How do you think your air conditioner stopped to begin with? If you want your little boyfriend here," she grabbed his arm and dug her nails into his skin, "you will give me the Pearl and go peacefully. Or . . ." She snapped her fingers. In unison, every mammoth skeleton took one giant step forward.

"Olivia! I'm sorry! Run!" Doug yelled out before Miss Rinkle clamped her hand over his mouth.

The bears couldn't hold out any longer. Three of them leapt toward the closest mammoth skeleton and clambered up over its back, swiping at the bones with their paws and biting down on any spot not covered with armor. The mammoth fought back. It swung its trunk and grabbed one of the bears by the leg. The sharp spikes on the end of the trunk dug into the bear's flesh. He let out a yelp of pain as the mammoth flung him into the water.

Now all of the other bears jumped into action. The entire cave shook with the great battle. Hoolie twitched angrily. More than anything he wanted to join his friends and fight these horrible creatures. But he had to protect Olivia.

A gigantic collision boomed as two of the mammoths tumbled into each other. Their bones disarticulated and crumbled into a pile. Another mammoth stomped its foot onto the back of a bear.

"This is your fault, Olivia. This is all your fault!" the witch screamed above the chaos. The mammoth skeletons were winning. Olivia knew she had to do something. She reached into her backpack and pulled out the Pearl. Its glow flooded the battle scene with light. Doug squirmed in the witch's grip.

"Yes . . . yes," the Witch murmured. She leaned into Doug's ear. "Now I will eat you both."

Olivia opened the Pearl. She tried to block out the horrible sounds of the bears getting hurt so she could hear the music and open the right doors, switches, and hinges. *The platinum hinge? Where was it?* She couldn't find it anywhere. She must have made a mistake with one of the switches. A spinning light rose up from the Pearl. Inside the light, Olivia could see the mammoths with all their skin, back when they were truly alive, fighting their way through hundreds of strange little people. It was the past! The original battle for the Pearl!

Another bear yowled.

"Your time is up, Olivia," the witch yelled as a path opened between her and Hoolie. Every other bear was engaged with the mammoth warriors. In a few seconds, the portal to the past disappeared back into the Pearl. Olivia kept trying to find the platinum switch.

Doug fought with his hands but the witch was too strong. He couldn't bear to watch as the wooly mammoth approached Olivia. So he bit down with his teeth. Hard.

"AAaaahhh Yoww!" the witch screamed.

"Syphlan ni manno wie," Doug yelled so loudly it rang through the cave, clear above the noise of the battle. The witch stopped in her tracks. She remembered those words. She recognized the sound of them.

"Y . . . You . . ." she stammered, turning toward him. "You . . . are . . . Junonian?" Her eyes opened almost wider than her head.

"Syphlan con bangan wie!" Doug yelled again, not even understanding what he was saying.

Olivia couldn't believe what she was seeing. Out of the darkness of the cave, from all directions, the enormous clear monsters that had attacked Squirt and the urchins walked into view. The tardigrades were marching toward the battle. Doug really *could* command them! They immediately attacked the mammoths, knocking them off their bony legs. Recognizing the help, the bears fought with renewed energy. The battle turned in their favor. The violence thundered through the ground with a terrible shaking. Squirt quivered with fear in Olivia's pocket.

Gnat yelled, "Crush them!"

"Crogan Horses! But . . . but . . . I am helping your people . . . your legacy!" the witch was still in shock. She hadn't heard the Junonian language for thousands of years. "You are now a Dark Eye," she snarled. Her face darkened with the thick red stripe across her eyes. Seeing how the battle had turned against her, she leapt from the back of the mammoth and ran toward Olivia. Doug jumped and grabbed her legs but she shook free. The Pearl was right there! So close! Her arms seemed to stretch out longer and longer. Only a few more steps and it would be hers.

Suddenly, out of the darkness, a huge paw swung, knocking the witch far out into the deep water. Hoolie finally had his chance to fight. He shook the kids from his back so he could rush after the witch. Olivia's fingers slipped and turned a switch inside the Pearl just as it tumbled from her hands.

The witch saw her chance. She started to swim toward the shallows . . . only . . . she couldn't. She was stuck. The underground lake surrounding the tombolo was freezing solid — she was trapped!

"Olivia! You only have five seconds to reverse the law! Switch it back, you don't understand what . . ." The witch's last words faded away as only the top of her head remained above the ice.

Olivia panicked. The realization rushed through her. When gravity disappeared in her bedroom, she *had* switched it back within five seconds. The Pearl gives you a single chance to correct a wrong choice! Her fingers fumbled around inside the Pearl. She couldn't remember which one she had hit. She paused. Five seconds had long since passed. She had permanently increased the transitional temperatures of water. Water no longer froze at 32 degrees Fahrenheit. The cave was only 68 degrees and that was cold enough to freeze all of the water!

The ice spread through the lake. Bears jumped out of the water and onto the sand just in time. The giant tardigrades curled themselves into balls and rolled back into the caves. Too slow, the mammoth skeletons were trapped. The spell that the witch had cast was broken and the mammoths collapsed into giant piles of bones onto the ice. The water in the bear's fur and kids' hair froze solid.

The battle was over.

"Dougie!" Gnat ran over to his friend.

"Hello, Acorn Chucker." Doug hugged him. "Thanks for coming for me."

Olivia walked out onto the ice. One thing she did remember from living in Wisconsin was how to walk efficiently on ice. She looked down at the top of Miss Rinkle's head. It occurred to her just how *much* she had wanted Miss Rinkle to like her. How nice it was to have a woman care for her and tell her how smart she was. Through the clear ice, she could see Miss Rinkle's face frozen solid like it was still screaming. Olivia wondered what she had been trying to say.

Nestled in Miss Rinkle's now frozen hair, the red birthday barrette

sparkled. Reaching down, Olivia carefully unclipped the barrette and held it in her hand. The tiny bumblebee flew from one flower to the next. This barrette had brought her nothing but trouble. Maybe all of this would have happened anyway. But the *way* it happened was the worst part. Maybe their Dad wouldn't have disappeared if the witch hadn't sent the barrette. Olivia ran her fingers through her own hair, then bent down and put the barrette back on the witch's head. It is hers. Let it bring *her* trouble.

"I guess we didn't know who Miss Rinkle really was," Doug said behind her.

"She was the Bobwhite Witch," Olivia responded.

"Uh . . . there are no such things as the Bobwhite Witch," Doug said, "I told you."

Olivia just shook her head as they walked past the mammoth warrior bones to begin the long journey home.

22

Consequences

The forest that the kids climbed into from the tortoise burrow staircase was a vastly different world than the one they had left. Hurricane Alphonse had devastated the trees, ripping off almost every branch and leaf. The entire forest consisted only of tree trunks. Destruction surrounded them. Butterflies were everywhere, but the air felt weird. Little puddles of ice were slowly melting in the hot morning sun. Their hair and clothes started to drip.

It suddenly occurred to Olivia that she actually had changed a law of nature everywhere in the world, not just in the cave. Water now froze at 68 degrees. Doug knelt down and lifted up an entire puddle in his hands.

"It's warm!" he exclaimed.

"Yeah," said Gnat touching the thin slab. "It feels like plastic."

Olivia's mind churned. "Water freezes at a higher temperature now."

"Ice doesn't need to be cold anymore!" Doug yelled out. Sometimes during very cold winters there would be frost on his mother's windshield, but he had never seen anything like this.

"Warm ice!" yelled Gnat.

Olivia refused to ride the bears back to the Milligans' house. So many of them were hurt. They didn't need to be carrying her around too. As they walked, she told Doug and Gnat the entire story. From the men attacking her at the gas station, to the shells and birds on the beach, to her accidentally turning off gravity, to the Bobwhite Witch and Miss Rinkle, to the stories that Uncle had told her. Long gone was the little girl who ran into the woods wearing flip-flops and harassed an innocent tortoise. Long gone was the little girl dreaming of becoming a ballerina. Olivia was a bear charmer and the *Guardian*. Everyone was depending on her. As she thought about it and walked along the bear highway, she realized that Hoolie and the bears were following *her* through the woods. She knew her own way through the secret highways.

As they got closer to the house, Olivia started figuring out how they were going to free Aunt and Uncle from those men. Maybe the bears couldn't fight very hard, but they could sure scare them. The bears waited back in the woods as they approached the house.

They walked up to the fence line. The hair on Olivia's neck stood up. Something wasn't right. There was no fence! She looked over to the side. The walkingstick church was gone. Aunt's garden was nothing but a patch of sand. Even the goldfish pond had disappeared. Gnat stared at the flat clearing of sand where the Milligans' house used to be. There was no sign that a house once stood there. Olivia's heart sank. What had she done? Had she wiped away the existence of her entire family? Even the enormous opal boulder was missing.

Suddenly, a muddy, exhausted dachshund stormed out of the woods and leapt into their arms. Cheeto was so happy to see Olivia! He licked her all over the face and told her in dog language just how special he felt to be loved by her.

"Ahhh . . . baybeee. You are okay now!" Olivia said.

"Where did it go?" Doug asked.

"I have no clue. Maybe the hurricane?"

"There would be stuff all over if it was the hurricane," Doug said, remembering the last time he saw the destruction from a storm.

A glinting spark caught Olivia's eye. She walked onto the sand to the exact center of the house, if there had indeed been a house there. Half-buried in the sand shone a small beetle fashioned out of polished silver and a strange grass-green metal. Olivia reached down and picked it up. It was incredible. The workmanship was so precise that the beetle looked like it would fly away from her hand.

"I wonder what this is," she said, stringing it onto her coral snake beads.

"Mom!" Doug yelled out. Just as he saw her pull up in her old sedan he realized that perhaps it wasn't only the Milligan house that had disappeared. To his relief, his mother seemed safe.

"Doug! You are all right! Hallelujah!" she screamed with delight. "What happened here?" she asked. "Where were you?"

"Olivia and Gnat saved me. They came out into the storm to look for me."

"Oh, dear. Thank you so much. You are angels. I am so sorry I was mean to you earlier." Mrs. Corcoran beamed, tears streaming down her cheeks. "But where are the Milligans? Where is your home?" The horror of the situation flashed across her face.

"Come children, you are all coming home with us until we figure this out," she said, opening the car door. Cheeto leapt into the back seat. Mrs. Corcoran smiled. "You too!"

On the ride back to the Corcorans', Olivia pressed her forehead into the window. Words and voices were racing through her mind:

grave responsibility

I can even help you find your father and mother

always say yes to the possibilities

Sky Island!

good people have to find it before the bad people do

Those words rolled around and made a nuisance of themselves. The car radio crackled with anxious news about a world water crisis and an atmosphere devoid of water vapor. A severe worldwide drought would ensue if something didn't change. The world's foremost experts were working around the clock trying to understand why the transitional temperature of water suddenly changed. Many suspected rising carbon levels in our air.

Olivia remembered Uncle bravely claiming to be the Guardian to protect her, even after she had been so rude to him. Things had spun out of control. It was too much for Olivia to figure out. But she did know she couldn't let the Cult of Wardenclyffe attack Doug and Gnat like they had Aunt and Uncle. She put her hand in her pocket and stroked Squirt's back. How was he going to survive without the rain? How would any of them?

For the second time that summer, Olivia and Gnat entered a new home. The curtains were mustard yellow and the carpeting was a strange green color. Everything was old and out of date. As they slowly walked around the corner, the only modern thing in the whole house came into view. It was a gigantic, flat-screen television dominating the living room. A bookcase next to the television overflowed with every video game they could imagine. Gnat's eyes teared up and he sat down to stare at the enormous blank screen. Cheeto ran around sniffing every delicious corner of the house.

That night, Olivia sat on her new bed. She was writing on a piece of paper with an incredibly large pencil that Doug had won at the Catkin County Fair last year by inflating a balloon with a water pistol faster than anyone else. In the dark house, she quietly padded her way down the hallway and snuck into Doug's room. She placed the note on his nightstand. Gnat was sleeping on the top bunk. Olivia climbed up the ladder and kissed him on his huge, bald forehead.

In the kitchen, she turned on the faucet. Only a small trickle came out. She filled up a thermos and dunked Squirt in the last of the dripping.

"Squeak!" he called out.

"Ssshhhh," Olivia whispered. But the noise was enough to wake Doug. He sat up and noticed the note. He turned on his light and read:

Dear Doug,

> *Please take care of Gnat and Cheeto. I have to go find Uncle and Aunt. I have to find rain. Tell Gnat I love him. Do not worry, I will return the thermos.*

Olivia

P.S. You are not a nerd. You are a genius.

He leapt out of bed with a scream. "Olivia!" he yelled, turning on every light in the house. His mother came running. Gnat awoke with a start. The back door creaked. "Olivia!" Doug ran to the door. Just as he looked out into the blackness between the neighborhood streetlights, he saw a brown-haired girl with a backpack riding a cinnamon-tufted bear into the woods. A faint blue glow followed her, fading into the dark.

Here are some other titles from Pineapple Press. To request a catalog or to place an order, write to Pineapple Press, P.O. Box 3889, Sarasota, Florida 34230, or call 1-800-PINEAPL (746-3275). Or visit our website at www.pineapplepress.com.

Solomon by Marilyn Bishop Shaw. Young Solomon Freeman and his parents, Moses and Lela, survive the Civil War, gain their freedom, and gamble their dreams, risking their very existence on a homestead in the remote environs of north central Florida. (hb)

Blood Moon Rider by Zack C. Waters. When his Marine father is killed in WWII, young Harley Wallace is exiled to the Florida cattle ranch of his grandfather. A murder and kidnapping lead Harley and his friend Beth on a wild ride through the swamps to solve a mystery linked to the war. (hb)

Escape to the Everglades by Edwina Raffa and Annelle Rigsby. Based on historical fact, this young adult novel tells the story of Will Cypress, a half-Seminole boy living among his mother's people during the Second Seminole War. He meets Chief Osceola and travels with him to St. Augustine. (hb)

Kidnapped in Key West by Edwina Raffa and Annelle Rigsby. Twelve-year-old Eddie Malone is living in the Florida Keys in 1912 when his world is turned upside down. His father, a worker on Henry Flagler's Over-Sea Railroad, is thrown into jail for stealing the railroad payroll. Eddie sets out for Key West with his faithful dog, Rex, on a daring mission to prove his father's innocence. Can he escape from the clutches of the ruthless thieves? Will he ever get back home? (hb)

A Land Remembered: Student Edition by Patrick D. Smith. This well-loved, best-selling novel tells the story of three generations of the MacIveys, a Florida family battling the hardships of the frontier, and how they rise from a dirt-poor Cracker life to the wealth and standing of real estate tycoons. Now available to young readers in two volumes. (hb & pb)

The Spy Who Came In from the Sea by Peggy Nolan. In 1943 14-year-old Frank Holleran sees an enemy spy land on Jacksonville Beach. First Frank needs to get people to believe him, and then he needs to stop the spy from carrying out his dangerous plans. Winner of the Sunshine State Young Reader's Award. (hb & pb)

The Treasure of Amelia Island by M.C. Finotti. Mary Kingsley, the youngest child of former slave Ana Jai Kingsley, recounts the life-changing events of December 1813. Her family lives in La Florida, a Spanish territory under siege by patriots who see no place for freed people of color in a new Florida. Against these mighty events, Mary decides to search for a legendary pirate treasure with her brothers. This treasure hunt, filled with danger and recklessness, changes Mary forever. (hb)